THE GOVERN...
OF SECTOR ALPHA CRUCIS

was breathing hard, anticipating his final
triumph over the rebel woman he had degraded.

'Where is she?' he demanded.

'This way, sir,' Flandry said. He followed
the Governor through the long corridors of
the ship to the room where the prisoner was
kept.

Flandry opened the door and stepped back.
'I brought you a visitor, Kathryn,' he said.

*She uttered a noise that would long run through
his nightmares. The Merseian war knife he had
given her flashed in her hand.*

Flandry kicked the door shut and pinned the
governor's arms behind him. 'Any way you
choose, Kathryn,' he said. 'Anyway at all.'

**The Governor of Sector Alpha Crucis
began screaming.**

Also by the same author
The Enemy Stars
and available in Coronet Books

The
Rebel Worlds

Poul Anderson

CORONET BOOKS
Hodder Paperbacks Ltd., London

Copyright © 1969 by Poul Anderson
First published 1969 by Signet Books, New York
Coronet edition 1972

Printed and bound in Great Britain for
Coronet Books, Hodder Paperbacks Ltd,
St. Paul's House, Warwick Lane,
London, E.C.4
By Hunt Barnard Printing Ltd,
Aylesbury, Bucks.

ISBN 0 340 16338 0

M̲ake oneness.

I/we: Feet belonging to Guardian Of North Gate and others who can be, to Raft Farer and Woe who will no longer be, to Many Thoughts, Cave Discoverer, and Master Of Songs who can no longer be; Wings belonging to Iron Miner and Lightning Struck The House and others to be, to Many Thoughts who can no longer be; young Hands that has yet to share memories: make oneness.

(O light, wind, river! They flood too strongly, they tear me/us apart.)

Strength. This is not the first young Hands which has come here to remember the journey that was made so many years before he/she was born; nor shall this be the last. Think strength, think calm.

(Blurred, two legs, faceless . . . no, had they beaks?)

Remember. Lie down at ease where leaves whisper beneath hues of upthrusting land coral; drink light and wind and sound of the river. Let reminiscence flow freely, of deeds that were done before this my/our Hands came to birth.

(Clearer, now: so very strange they were, how can the sight of them even be seen, let alone held in me/us? . . . Answer: The eye learns to see them, the nose to smell them, the ear to hear them, the tongue of the Feet and the limbs of the Wings and the Hands to touch their skins and feel, the tendrils to taste what they exude.)

This goes well. More quickly than usual. Perhaps i/we can become a good oneness that will often have reason to exist.

(Flicker of joy. Tide of terror at the rising memories—alienness, peril, pain, death, rebirth to torment.)

Lie still. It was long ago.

5

But time too is one. Now is unreal; only past-and-future has the length to be real. What happened then must be known to Us. Feel in every fiber of my/our young Hands, that i/we am/are part of Us—We of Thunderstone, Ironworkers, Fellers and Builders, Plowers, Housedwellers, and lately Traders—and that each oneness We may create must know of those who come from beyond heaven, lest their dangerous marvels turn into Our ruin.

Wherefore let Hands unite with Feet and Wings. Let the oneness once again recall and reflect on the journey of Cave Discoverer and Woe, in those days when the strangers, who had but single bodies and yet could talk, marched overmountain to an unknown battle. With every such reflection, as with every later encounter, i/we gain a little more insight, go a little further along the trail that leads to understanding them.

Though it may be that on that trail, We are traveling in a false direction. The unit who led them said on a certain night that he/she/it/? doubted if they understood themselves, or ever would.

I

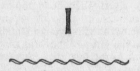

The prison satellite swung in a wide and canted orbit around Llynathawr, well away from normal space traffic. Often a viewport in Hugh McCormac's cell showed him the planet in different phases. Sometimes it was a darkness, touched with red-and-gold sunrise on one edge, perhaps the city Catawrayannis flickering like a star upon its night. Sometimes it was a scimitar, the sun burning dazzlingly close. Now and then he saw it full, a round shield of brilliance, emblazoned on oceans azure with clouds argent above continents vert and tenné.

Terra looked much the same at the same distance. (Closer

6

in, you became aware that she was haggard, as is any former beauty who has been used by too many men.) But Terra was a pair of light-centuries removed. And neither world resembled rusty, tawny Aeneas for which McCormac's eyes hungered.

The satellite had no rotation; interior weight was due entirely to gravity-field generators. However, its revolution made heaven march slowly across the viewport. When Llynathawr and sun had disappeared, a man's pupils readjusted and he became able to see other stars. They crowded space, unwinking, jewel-colored, winter-sharp. Brightest shone Alpha Crucis, twin blue-white giants less than ten parsecs away; but Beta Crucis, a single of the same kind, was not much further off in its part of the sky. Elsewhere, trained vision might identify the red glimmers of Aldebaran and Arcturus. They resembled fires which, though remote, warmed and lighted the camps of men. Or vision might swing out to Deneb and Polaris, unutterably far beyond the Empire and the Empire's very enemies. That was a cold sight.

Wryness tugged at McCormac's mouth. *If Kathryn were tuned in on my mind,* he thought, *she'd say there must be something in Leviticus against mixing so many metaphors.*

He dared not let the knowledge of her dwell with him long. *I'm lucky to have an outside cell. Not uncomfortable, either. Surely this wasn't Snelund's intention.*

The assistant warden had been as embarrassed and apologetic as he dared. "We, uh, well, these are orders for us to detain you, Admiral McCormac," he said. "Direct from the governor. Till your trial or . . . transportation to Terra, maybe . . . uh . . . till further orders." He peered at the fax on his desk, conceivably hoping that the words it bore had changed since his first perusal. "Uh, solitary confinement, incommunicado—state-of-emergency powers invoked—Frankly, Admiral McCormac, I don't see why you aren't allowed, uh, books, papers, even projections to pass the time. . . . I'll send to His Excellency and ask for a change."

I know why, McCormac had thought. *Partly spite; mainly, the initial stage in the process of breaking me.* His back grew yet stiffer. *Well, let them try!*

The sergeant of the housecarl platoon that had brought the prisoner up from Catawrayannis Port said in his brassiest voice, "Don't address traitors by titles they've forfeited."

The assistant warden sat bolt upright, nailed them all with a look, and rapped: "Sergeant, I was twenty years in the Navy before retiring to my present job. I made CPO. Under His Majesty's regulations, any officer of Imperials ranks every

7

member of any paramilitary local force. Fleet Admiral McCormac may have been relieved of command, but unless and until he's decommissioned by a proper court-martial or by direct fiat from the throne, you'll show him respect or find yourself in worse trouble than you may already be in."

Flushed, breathing hard, he seemed to want to say more. Evidently he thought better of it. After a moment, during which a couple of the burly guards shifted from foot to foot, he added merely: "Sign the prisoner over to me and get out."

"We're supposed to—" the sergeant began.

"If you have written orders to do more than deliver this gentleman into custody, let's see them." Pause. "Sign him over and get out. I don't plan to tell you again."

McCormac placed the assistant warden's name and face in his mind as carefully as he had noted each person involved in his arrest. Someday—if ever—

What had become of the man's superior? McCormac didn't know. Off Aeneas, he had never been concerned with civilian crime or penology. The Navy looked after its own. Sending him here was an insult tempered only by the fact that obviously it was done to keep him away from brother officers who'd try to help him. McCormac guessed that Snelund had replaced a former warden with a favorite or a bribegiver—as he'd done to many another official since he became sector governor—and that the new incumbent regarded the post as a sinecure.

In any case, the admiral was made to exchange his uniform for a gray coverall; but he was allowed to do so in a booth. He was taken to an isolation cell; but although devoid of ornament and luxury, it had room for pacing and facilities for rest and hygiene. The ceiling held an audiovisual scanner; but it was conspicuously placed, and no one objected when he rigged a sheet curtain for his bunk. He saw no other being, heard no other voice; but edible food and clean fabrics came in through a valve, and he had a chute for disposal of scraps and soils. Above all else, he had the viewport.

Without that sun, planet, constellations, frosty rush of Milky Way and dim gleam of sister galaxies, he might soon have crumbled—screamed for release, confessed to anything, kissed the hand of his executioner, while honest medics reported to headquarters on Terra that they had found no sign of torture or brainscrub upon him. It would not have been the sensory deprivation *per se* that destroyed his will in such short order. It would have been the loss of every distraction from the thought of Kathryn, every way of guessing how long a time had gone by while she also lay in Aaron Sne-

8

lund's power. McCormac admitted the weakness to himself. That was not one he was ashamed of.

Why hadn't the governor then directed he be put in a blank cell? Oversight, probably, when more urgent business demanded attention. Or, being wholly turned inward on himself, Snelund perhaps did not realize that other men might love their wives above life.

Of course, as day succeeded standard day (with never a change in this bleak white fluorescence) he must begin wondering why nothing had happened up here. If his observers informed him of the exact situation, no doubt he would prescribe that McCormac be shifted to different quarters. But agents planted in the guard corps of a small artificial moon were lowly creatures. They would not, as a rule, report directly to a sector governor, viceroy for His Majesty throughout some 50,000 cubic light-years surrounding Alpha Crucis, and a *very* good friend of His Majesty to boot. No, they wouldn't even when the matter concerned a fleet admiral, formerly responsible for the defense of that entire part of the Imperial marches.

Petty agents would report to administrative underlings, who would send each communication on its way through channels. Was somebody seeing to it that material like this got—no, not lost—shunted off to oblivion in the files?

McCormac sighed. The noise came loud across endless whisper of ventilation, clack of his shoes on metal. How long could such protection last?

He didn't know the satellite's orbit. Nevertheless, he could gauge the angular diameter of Llynathawr pretty closely. He remembered the approximate dimensions and mass. From that he could calculate radius vector and thus period. Not easy, applying Kepler's laws in your head, but what else was there to do? The result more or less confirmed his guess that he was being fed thrice in 24 hours. He couldn't remember exactly how many meals had come before he started tallying them with knots in a thread. Ten? Fifteen? Something like that. Add this to the 37 points now confronting him. You got between 40 and 50 spaceship watches; or 13 to 16 Terran days; or 15 to 20 Aenean.

Aenean. The towers of Windhome, tall and gray, their banners awake in a whistling sky; tumble of crags and cliffs, reds, ochers, bronzes, where the Ilian Shelf plunged to a blue-gray dimness sparked and veined with watergleams, that was the Antonine Seabed; clangor of the Wildfoss as it hurled itself thitherward in cataracts; and Kathryn's laughter when

9

they rode forth, her gaze upon him more blue than the daz-
zlingly high sky—

"No!" he exclaimed. "Ramona's eyes had been blue. Kathryn's were green. Was he already confusing his live wife with
his dead one?

If he had a wife any more. Twenty days since the housecarls burst into their bedchamber, arrested them and took
them down separate corridors. She had slapped their hands
off her wrists and marched among their guns with scornful
pride, though tears rivered over her face.

McCormac clasped his hands and squeezed them together
till fingerbones creaked. The pain was a friend. *I mustn't,* he
recalled. *If I wring myself out because of what I can't make
better, I'm doing Snelund's work for him.*

What else can I do?

Resist. Until the end.

Not for the first time, he summoned the image of a being
he had once known, a Wodenite, huge, scaly, tailed, four-
legged, saurian-snouted, but comrade in arms and wiser than
most. "You humans are a kittle breed," the deep voice had
rumbled. "Together you can show courage that may cross the
threshold of madness. Yet when no one else is near to tell
your fellows afterward how you died, the spirit crumbles
away and you fall down empty."

"Heritage of instinct, I suppose," McCormac said. "Our
race began as an animal that hunted in packs."

"Training can tame instinct," the dragon answered. "Can
the intelligent mind not train itself?"

Alone in his cell, Hugh McCormac nodded. *I've at least
got that damned monitor to watch me. Maybe someday
somebody—Kathryn, or the children Ramona gave me, or
some boy I never knew—will see its tapes.*

He lay down on his bunk, the sole furnishing besides washbasin and sanitizer, and closed his eyes. *I'll try playing mental
chess again, alternating sides, till dinner. Give me enough
time and I'll master the technique. Just before eating, I'll
have another round of calisthenics. That drab mess in the
soft bowl won't suffer from getting cold. Perhaps later I'll be
able to sleep.*

He hadn't lowered his improvised curtain. The pickup recorded a human male, tall, rangy, more vigorous than could
be accounted for by routine antisenescence. Little betrayed
his 50-standard years except the grizzling of black hair and
the furrows in his long, lean countenance. He had never
changed those features, nor protected them from the weath-
ers of many planets. The skin remained dark and leathery. A

jutting triangle of nose, a straight mouth and lantern jaw, were like counterweights to the dolichocephalic skull. When he opened the eyes beneath his heavy brows, they would show the color of glaciers. When he spoke, his voice tended to be hard; and decades of service around the Empire, before he returned to his home sector, had worn away the accent of Aeneas.

He lay there, concentrating so furiously on imagined chessmen which kept slipping about like fog-wraiths, that he did not notice the first explosion. Only when another went *crump!* and the walls reverberated did he know it was the second.

"What the chaos?" He surged to his feet.

A third detonation barked dully and toned in metal. *Heavy slugthrowers,* he knew. Sweat spurted forth. The heart slammed within him. What had happened? He threw a glance at the viewport. Llynathawr was rolling into sight, unmarked, serene, indifferent.

A rushing noise sounded at the door. A spot near its molecular catch glowed red, then white. Somebody was cutting through with a blaster. Voices reached McCormac, indistinct but excited and angry. A slug went *bee-yowww* down the corridor, gonged off a wall, and dwindled to nothing.

The door wasn't thick, just sufficient to contain a man. Its alloy gave way, streamed downward, made fantastic little formations akin to lava. The blaster flame boomed through the hole, enlarging it. McCormac squinted away from that glare. Ozone prickled his nostrils. He thought momentarily, crazily, *no reason to be so extravagant of charge.*

The gun stopped torching. The door flew wide. A dozen beings stormed through. Most were men in blue Navy outfits. A couple of them bulked robotlike in combat armor and steered a great Holbert energy gun on its grav sled. One was nonhuman, a Donarrian centauroid, bigger than the armored men themselves; he bore an assortment of weapons on his otherwise nude frame, but had left them holstered in favor of a battleax. It dripped red. His simian countenance was a single vast grin.

"Admiral! Sir!" McCormac didn't recognize the youth who dashed toward him, hands outspread. "Are you all right?"

"Yes. Yes. What—" McCormac willed out bewilderment. "What is this?"

The other snapped a salute. "Lieutenant Nasruddin Hamid, sir, commanding your rescue party by order of Captain Oliphant."

11

"Assaulting an Imperial installation?" It was as if somebody else used McCormac's larynx.

"Sir, they meant to kill you. Captain Oliphant's sure of it." Hamid looked frantic. "We've got to move fast, sir. We entered without loss. The man in charge knew about the operation. He pulled back most of the guards. He'll leave with us. A few disobeyed him and resisted. Snelund's men, must be. We cut through them but some escaped. They'll be waiting to send a message soon's our ships stop jamming."

The event was still unreal for McCormac. Part of him wondered if his mind had ripped across. "Governor Snelund was appointed by His Majesty," jerked from his gullet. "The proper place to settle things is a court of inquiry."

Another man trod forth. He had not lost the lilt of Aeneas. "Please, sir." He was near weeping. "We can't do without you. Local uprisin's on more planets every day—on ours, now, too, in Borea and Ironland. Snelund's tryin' to get the Navy to help his filthy troops put down the trouble . . . by his methods . . . by nuclear bombardment if burnin', shootin', and enslavin' don't work."

"War on our own people," McCormac whispered, "when outside the border, the barbarians—"

His gaze drifted back to Llynathawr, aglow in the port. "What about my wife?"

"I don't . . . don't know . . . anything about her—" Hamid stammered.

McCormac swung to confront him. Rage leaped aloft. He grabbed the lieutenant's tunic. "That's a lie!" he yelled. "You can't help knowing! Oliphant wouldn't send men on a raid without briefing them on every last detail. *What about Kathryn?*"

"Sir, the jamming'll be noticed. We only have a surveillance vessel. An enemy ship on picket could—"

McCormac shook Hamid till teeth rattled in the jaws. Abruptly he let go. They saw his face become a machine's. "What touched off part of the trouble was Snelund's wanting Kathryn," he said, altogether toneless. "The Governor's court likes its gossip juicy; and what the court knows, soon all Catawrayannis does. She's still in the palace, isn't she?"

The men looked away, anywhere except at him. "I heard that," Hamid mumbled. "Before we attacked, you see, we stopped at one of the asteroids—pretended we were on a routine relief—and sounded out whoever we could. One was a merchant, come from the city the day before. He said—well, a public announcement about you, sir, and your lady being 'detained for investigation,' only she and the governor—"

12

He stopped.

After a while, McCormac reached forth and squeezed his shoulder. "You needn't continue, son," he said, with scarcely more inflection but quite softly. "Let's board your ship."

"We aren't mutineers, sir," Hamid said pleadingly. "We need you to—to hold off that monster . . . till we can get the truth before the Emperor."

"No, it can't be called mutiny any longer," McCormac answered. "It has to be revolt." His voice whipped out. "Get moving! On the double!"

II

A metropolis in its own right, Admiralty Center lifted over that part of North America's Rocky Mountains which it occupied, as if again the Titans of dawn myth were piling Pelion on Ossa to scale Olympus. "And one of these days," Dominic Flandry had remarked to a young woman whom he was showing around, and to whom he had made that comparison in order to demonstrate his culture, "the gods are going to get as irritated as they did last time—let us hope with less deplorable results."

"What do you mean?" she asked.

Because his objective was not to enlighten but simply to seduce her, he had twirled his mustache and leered: "I mean that you are far too lovely for me to exercise my doomsmanship on. Now as for that plotting tank you wanted to see, this way, please."

He didn't tell her that its spectacular three-dimensional star projections were mainly for visitors. The smallest astronomical distance is too vast for any pictorial map to have much value. The real information was stored in the memory banks of unpretentious computers which the general public was not allowed to look on.

As his cab entered the area today, Flandry recalled the little episode. It had terminated satisfactorily. But his mind would not break free of the parallel he had not uttered.

Around him soared many-tinted walls, so high that fluoropanels must glow perpetually on the lower levels, a liana tangle of elevated ways looping between them, the pinnacles crowned with clouds and sunlight. Air traffic swarmed and glittered in their sky, a dance too dense and complex for anything but electronic brains to control; and traffic pulsed among the towers, up and down within them, deep into the tunnels and chambers beneath their foundations. Those cars and buses, airborne or ground, made barely a whisper; likewise the slideways; and a voice or a footfall was soon lost. Nevertheless, Admiralty Center stood in a haze of sound, a night-and-day hum like a beehive's above an undergroundish growling, the noise of its work.

For here was the nexus of Imperial strength; and Terra ruled a rough sphere some 400 light-years across, containing an estimated four million suns, of which a hundred thousand were in one way or another tributary to her.

Thus far the pride. When you looked behind it, though—

Flandry emerged from his reverie. His cab was slanting toward Intelligence headquarters. He took a hasty final drag on his cigaret, pitched it in the disposer, and checked his uniform. He preferred the dashing dress version, with as much elegant variation as the rather elastic rules permitted, or a trifle more. However, when your leave has been cancelled after a mere few days Home, and you are ordered to report straight to Vice Admiral Kheraskov, you had better arrive in plain white tunic and trousers, the latter not tucked into your half-boots, and belt instead of sash, and simple gray cloak, and bonnet cocked to bring its sunburst badge precisely over the middle of your forehead.

Sackcloth and ashes would be more appropriate, Flandry mourned. *Three, count 'em, three gorgeous girls, ready and eager to help me celebrate my birth week, starting tomorrow at Everest House with a menu I spent two hours planning; and we'd've continued as long as necessary to prove that a quarter century is less old than it sounds. And now this!*

A machine in the building talked across seething communications to a machine in the cab. Flandry was deposited on the fiftieth-level parking flange. The gravs cut out. He lent his card to the meter, which transferred credit and unlocked the door for him. A marine guard at the entrance verified his

14

identity and appointment with the help of another machine and let him through. He passed down several halls on his way to the lift shaft he wanted. Restless, he walked in preference to letting a strip carry him.

Crowds moved by and overflowed the offices. Their members ranged from junior technicians to admirals on whose heads might rest the security of a thousand worlds and scientists who barely kept the Empire afloat in a universe full of lethal surprises. By no means all were human. Shapes, colors, words, odors, tactile sensations when he brushed against a sleeve or an alien skin, swirled past Flandry in endless incomprehensible patterns.

Hustle, bustle, hurry, scurry, run, run, run, said his glumness. *Work, for the night is coming—the Long Night, when the Empire goes under and the howling peoples camp in its ruins. Because how can we remain forever the masters, even of our insignificant spatter of stars, on the fringe of a galaxy so big we'll never know a decent fraction of it? Probably never more than this sliver of one spiral arm that we've already seen. Why, better than half the suns, just in the microbubble of space we claim, have not been visited once!*

Our ancestors explored further than we in these years remember. When hell cut loose and their civilization seemed about to fly into pieces, they patched it together with the Empire. And they made the Empire function. But we . . . we've lost the will. We've had it too easy for too long. And so the Merseians on our Betelgeusean flank, the wild races everywhere else, press inward. . . . Why do I bother? Once a career in the Navy looked glamorous to me. Lately I've seen its backside. I could be more comfortable doing almost anything else.

A woman stopped him. She must be on incidental business, because civilian employees here couldn't get away with dressing in quite such a translucent wisp of rainbow. She was constructed for it. "I beg your pardon," she said. "Could you tell me how to find Captain Yuan-Li's office? I'm afraid I'm lost."

Flandry bowed. "Indeed, my lady." He had reported in there on arrival at Terra, and now directed her. "Please tell him Lieutenant Commander Flandry said he's a lucky captain."

She fluttered her lashes. "Oh, sir." Touching the insigne on his breast, a star with an eye: "I noticed you're in Intelligence. That's why I asked you. It must be fascinating. I'd love to—"

15

Flandry beamed. "Well, since we both know friend Yuan-Li—"

They exchanged names and addresses. She departed, wagging her tail. Flandry continued. His mood was greatly lightened. *After all, another job might prove boring.* He reached his upbound point. *Here's where I get the shaft.* Stepping through the portal, he relaxed while the negagrav field lifted him.

Rather, he tried to relax, but did not succeed a hundred percent. Attractive women or no, a new-made lieutcom summoned for a personal interview with a subchief of operations is apt to find his tongue a little dry and his palms a little wet.

Catching a handhold, he drew himself out on the ninety-seventh level and proceeded down the corridor. Here dwelt a hush; the rare soft voices, the occasional whirr of a machine, only deepened for him the silence between these austere walls. What persons he met were of rank above his, their eyes turned elsewhere, their thoughts among distant suns. When he reached Kheraskov's suite of offices, the receptionist was nothing but a scanner and talkbox hooked to a computer too low-grade to be called a brain. More was not needed. Everybody unimportant got filtered out at an earlier stage. Flandry cooled his heels a mere five minutes before it told him to proceed through the inner door.

The room beyond was large, high-ceilinged, lushly carpeted. In one corner stood an infotriever and an outsize vidiphone, in another a small refreshment unit. Otherwise there were three or four pictures, and as many shelves for mementos of old victories. The rear wall was an animation screen; at present it held an image of Jupiter seen from an approaching ship, so vivid that newcomers gasped. He halted at an expanse of desktop and snapped a salute that nearly tore his arm off. "Lieutenant Commander Dominic Flandry, reporting as ordered, sir."

The man aft of the desk was likewise in plain uniform. He wore none of the decorations that might have blanketed his chest, save the modest jewel of knighthood that was harder to gain than a patent of nobility. But his nebula and star outglistened Flandry's ringed planet. He was short and squat, with tired pugdog features under bristly gray hair. His return salute verged on being sloppy. But Flandry's heartbeat accelerated.

"At ease," said Vice Admiral Sir Ilya Kheraskov. "Sit down. Smoke?" He shoved forward a box of cigars.

"Thank you, sir." Flandry collected his wits. He chose a cigar and made a production of starting it, while the chair

16

fitted itself around his muscles and subtly encouraged them to relax. "The admiral is most kind. I don't believe a better brand exists than Corona Australis." In fact, he knew of several: but these weren't bad. The smoke gave his tongue a love bite and curled richly by his nostrils.

"Coffee if you like," offered the master of perhaps a million agents through the Empire and beyond. "Or tea or jaine."

"No, thanks, sir."

Kheraskov studied him, wearily and apologetically; he felt X-rayed. "I'm sorry to break your furlough like this, Lieutenant Commander," the admiral said. "You must have been anticipating considerable overdue recreation. I see you have a new face."

They had never met before. Flandry made himself smile. "Well, yes, sir. The one my parents gave me had gotten monotonous. And since I was coming to Terra, where biosculp is about as everyday as cosmetics—" He shrugged.

Still that gaze probed him. Kheraskov saw an athlete's body, 184 centimeters tall, wide in the shoulders and narrow in the hips. From the white, tapered hands you might guess how their owner detested the hours of exercise he must spend in maintaining those cat-supple thews. His countenance had become straight of nose, high of cheekbones, cleft of chin. The mobile mouth and the eyes, changeable gray beneath slightly arched brows, were original. Speaking, he affected a hint of drawl.

"No doubt you're wondering why your name should have been plucked off the roster," Kheraskov said, "and why you should have been ordered straight here instead of to your immediate superior or Captain Yuan-Li."

"Yes, sir. I didn't seem to rate your attention."

"Nor were you desirous to." Kheraskov's chuckle held no humor. "But you've got it." He leaned back, crossed stumpy legs and bridged hairy fingers. "I'll answer your questions.

"First, why you, one obscure officer among tens of similar thousands? You may as well know, Flandry, if you don't already—though I suspect your vanity has informed you—to a certain echelon of the Corps, you aren't obscure. You wouldn't hold the rank you've got, at your age, if that were the case. No, we've taken quite an interest in you since the Starkad affair. That had to be hushed up, of course, but it was not forgotten. Your subsequent assignment to surveillance had intriguing consequences." Flandry could not totally suppress a tinge of alarm. Kheraskov chuckled again; it sounded like iron chains. "We've learned things that *you* hushed up. Don't worry . . . yet. Competent men are so heartbreakingly scarce these days, not to mention brilliant ones, that the Service keeps a blind eye handy for a broad range of escapades. You'll either be killed, young man, or you'll do something that will force us to step on you, or you'll go far indeed."

He drew breath before continuing: "The present business requires a maverick. I'm not letting out any great secret when I tell you the latest Merseian crisis is worse than the government admits to the citizens. It could completely explode on us. I think we can defuse it. For once, the Empire acted fast and decisively. But it demands we keep more than the bulk of our fleets out on that border, till the Merseians understand we mean business about not letting them take over Jihannath. Intelligence operations there have reached such a scale that the Corps is sucked dry of able field operatives elsewhere.

"And meanwhile something else has arisen, on the opposite side of our suzerainty. Something potentially worse than any single clash with Merseia." Kheraskov lifted a hand. "Don't imagine you're the only man we're sending to cope, or that you can contribute more than a quantum to our effort. Still, stretched as thin as we are, every quantum is to be treasured. It was your bad luck but the Empire's good luck . . . maybe . . . that you happened to check in on Terra last week. When I asked Files who might be available with the right qualifications, your reel was among a dozen that came back."

Flandry waited.

Kheraskov rocked forward. The last easiness dropped from him. A grim and bitter man spoke: "As for why you're reporting directly to me—this is one place where I know there isn't any spybug, and you are one person I think won't backstab me. I told you we need a maverick. I tell you in addition, you could suck around the court and repeat what I'm about to say. I'd be broken, possibly shot or enslaved. You'd get money, possibly a sycophant's preferment. I have to take the chance. Unless you know the entire situation, you'll be useless."

Flandry said with care, "I'm a skilled liar, sir, so you'd better take my word rather than my oath that I'm not a very experienced buglemouth."

"Ha!" Kheraskov sat quiet for several seconds. Then he jumped to his feet and started to pace back and forth, one fist hammering into the other palm. The words poured from him:

"You've been away. After Starkad, your visits to Terra

18

were for advanced training and the like. You must have been too busy to follow events at court. Oh, scandal, ribald jokes, rumor, yes, you've heard those. Who hasn't? But the meaningful news—Let me brief you.

"Three years, now, since poor old Emperor Georgios died and Josip III succeeded. Everybody knows what Josip is: too weak and stupid for his viciousness to be highly effective. We all assumed the Dowager Empress will keep him on a reasonably short leash while she lives. And he won't outlast her by much, the way he treats his organism. And he won't have children—not him! And the Policy Board, the General Staff, the civil service, the officers corps, the Solar and extra-Solar aristocracies . . . they hold more crooks and incompetents than they did in former days, but we have a few good ones left, a few. . . .

"I've told you nothing new, have I?" Flandry barely had time to shake his head. Kheraskov kept on prowling and talking. "I'm sure you made the same quiet evaluation as most informed citizens. The Empire is so huge that no one individual can do critical damage, no matter if he's theoretically all-powerful. Whatever harm came from Josip would almost certainly be confined to a relative handful of courtiers, politicians, plutocrats, and their sort, concentrated on and around Terra—no great loss. We've survived other bad Emperors.

"A logical judgment. Correct, no doubt, as far as it went. But it didn't go far enough. Even we who're close to the seat of power were surprised by Aaron Snelund. Ever hear of him?"

"No, sir," Flandry said.

"He kept out of the media," Kheraskov explained. "Censorship's efficient on this planet, if nothing else is. The court knew about him, and people like me did. But our data were incomplete.

"Later you'll see details. I want to give you the facts that aren't public. He was born 34 years ago on Venus, mother a prostitute, father unknown. That was in Sub-Lucifer, where you learn ruthlessness early or go down. He was clever, talented, charming when he cared to be. By his mid-teens he was a sensie actor here on Terra. I can see by hindsight how he must have planned, investigated Josip's tastes in depth, sunk his money into just the right biosculping and his time into acquiring just the right mannerisms. Once they met, it went smooth as gravitation. By the age of 25, Aaron Snelund had gone from only another catamite to the Crown Prince's favorite. His next step was to ease out key people and obtain their offices for those who were beholden to Snelund.

19

"It roused opposition. More than jealousy. Honest men worried about him becoming the power behind the crown when Josip succeeded. We heard mutters about assassination. I don't know if Josip and Snelund grew alarmed or if Snelund foresaw the danger and planned against it. At any rate, they must have connived.

"Georgios died suddenly, you recall. The following week Josip made Snelund a viscount and appointed him governor of Sector Alpha Crucis. Can you see how well calculated that was? Elevation to a higher rank would have kicked up a storm, but viscounts are a millo a thousand. However, it's sufficient for a major governorship. Many sectors would be too rich, powerful, close to home, or otherwise important. The Policy Board would not tolerate a man in charge of them who couldn't be trusted. Alpha Crucis is different."

Kheraskov slapped a switch. The fluoros went off. The breathtaking view of Jupiter, huge and banded among its moons, vanished. A trikon of the principal Imperial stars jumped into its place. Perhaps Kheraskov's rage demanded that he at least have something to point at. His blocky form stood silhouetted against a gem-hoard.

"Betelgeuse." He stabbed one finger at a red spark representing the giant sun which dominated the borderlands between the Terran and Merseian empires. "Where the war threat is. Now, Alpha Crucis."

His hand swept almost 100 degrees counterclockwise. The other hand turned a control, swinging the projection plane about 70 degrees south. Keenly flashed the B-type giants at that opposite end of Terra's domain, twinned Alpha and bachelor Beta of the Southern Cross. Little showed beyond them except darkness. It was not that the stars did not continue as richly strewn in those parts; it was that they lay where Terra's writ did not run, the homes of savages and of barbarian predators who had too soon gotten spacecraft and nuclear weapons; it was that they housed darkness.

Kheraskov traced the approximately cylindrical outline of the sector. "Here," he said, "is where war could really erupt."

Flandry dared say into the shadowed silence which followed, "Does the admiral mean the wild races are going to try a fresh incursion? But sir, I understood they were well in check. After the battle of—uh—I forget its name, but wasn't there a battle—"

"Forty-three years ago." Kheraskov sagged in the shoulders. "Too big, this universe," he said tiredly. "No one brain, no one species can keep track of everything. So we let the bad seed grow unnoticed until too late.

"Well." He straightened. "It was hard to see what harm Snelund could do yonder that was worth provoking a constitutional crisis to forestall. The region's as distant as they come among ours. It's not highly productive, not densely populated; its loyalty and stability are no more doubtful than most. There are only two things about it that count. One's the industrial rogue planet Satan. But that's an ancient possession of the Dukes of Hermes. They can be trusted to protect their own interests. Second is the sector's position as the shield between us and various raiders. But that means defense is the business of the fleet admiral; and we have—had—a particularly fine man in that post, one Hugh McCormac. You've never heard of him, but you'll get data.

"Of course Snelund would grow fat. What of it? A cento or two per subject per year, diverted from Imperial taxes, won't hurt any individual so badly he'll make trouble. But it will build a fortune to satisfy any normal greed. He'd retire in time to a life of luxury. Meanwhile the Navy and civil service would do all the real work as usual. Everyone was happy to get Snelund that cheaply off Terra. It's the kind of solution which has been reached again and again."

"Only this time," Flandry said lazily, "they forgot to allow for a bugger factor."

Kheraskov switched the map off, the fluoros on, and gave him a hard look. Flandry's return glance was bland and deferential. Presently the admiral said, "He left three years ago. Since then, increasing complaints have been received of extortion and cruelty. But no single person saw enough of those reports to stir action. And if he had, what could he do? You don't run an interstellar realm from the center. It isn't possible. The Imperium is hardly more than a policeman, trying to keep peace internal and external. Tribes, countries, planets, provinces are autonomous in most respects. The agony of millions of sentient beings, 200 light-years away, doesn't register on several trillion other sophonts elsewhere, or whatever the figure is. It can't. And we've too much else to worry about anyway.

"Think, though, what a governor of a distant region, who chose to abuse his powers, might do."

Flandry did, and lost his lightness.

"McCormac himself finally sent protests to Terra," Kheraskov plodded on. "A two-star admiral can get through. The Policy Board began talking about appointing a commission to investigate. Almost immediately after, a dispatch came from Snelund himself. He'd had to arrest McCormac for conspir-

acy to commit treason. He can do that, you know, and select
an interim high commander. The court-martial must be held
on a Naval base or vessel, by officers of suitable rank. But
with this Merseian crisis— Do you follow me?"

"Too damn well." Flandry's words fell muted.

"Provincial rebellions aren't unheard of," Kheraskov said.
"We can less afford one today than we could in the past."

He had stood looking down at the younger man, across his
desk. Turning, he stared into the grand vision of Jupiter that
had come back. "The rest you can find in the data tapes," he
said.

"What do you want me to do . . . sir?"

"As I told you, we're sending what undercover agents we
can spare, plus a few inspectors. With all that territory to
deal with, they'll take long to compile a true picture. Perhaps
fatally long. I want to try something in between also. A man
who can nose around informally but openly, with authoriza-
tions to flash when needed. The master of a warship, posted
to Llynathawr as a reinforcement, has standing. Governor
Snelund, for instance, has no ready way of refusing to see
him. At the same time, if she's not a capital ship, her skipper
isn't too blazing conspicuous."

"But I've never had a command, sir."

"Haven't you?"

Tactfully, Kheraskov did not watch while the implications
of that question sank in. He proceeded: "We've found an escort destroyer whose captain is slated for higher things. The
record says she has an able executive officer. That should free
your attention for your true job. You'd have gotten a ship
eventually, in the normal course of grooming you and testing
your capabilities. We like our field operatives to have a broad
background."

Not apt to be many broads in my background for a while,
passed through the back of Flandry's mind. He scarcely noticed or cared. Excitement bayed in him.

Kheraskov sat down again. "Go back to your place," he
said. "Pack up and check out. Report at 1600 hours to Rear
Admiral Yamaguchi. He'll provide you with quarters, tapes,
hypnos, synapse transforms, stimpills, every aid you need.
And you will need them. I want your information to be as
complete as mine, inside 48 hours. You will then report to
Mars Prime Base and receive your brevet commission as a
full commander. Your ship is in Mars orbit. Departure will
be immediate. I hope you can fake the knowledge of her you
don't have, until you've gathered it.

"If you acquit yourself well, we'll see about making that temporary rank permanent. If you don't, God help you and maybe God help me. Good luck, Dominic Flandry."

III

The third stop *Asieneuve* made on her way to Llynathawr was her final one. Flandry recognized the need for haste. In straight-line, flat-out hyperdrive his vessel would have taken slightly worse than two weeks to make destination. Perhaps he should have relied on records and interviews after he arrived. On the other hand, he might not be given the chance, or Snelund might have found ways to keep the truth off his headquarters planet. The latter looked feasible, therefore plausible. And Flandry's orders granted him latitude. They instructed him to report to Llynathawr and place himself under the new high command of Sector Alpha Crucis "with maximum expedition and to the fullest extent consistent with your fact-finding assignment." A sealed letter from Kheraskov authorized him to detach his ship and operate independently; but that must not be produced except in direst need, and he'd have to answer for his actions.

He compromised by making spot checks in three randomly chosen systems within Snelund's bailiwick and not too far off his course. It added an extra ten days. Two globes were human-colonized. The habitable planet of the third sun was Shalmu.

So it was called in one of the languages spoken by its most technologically advanced civilization. Those communities had been in a bronze age when men discovered them. Influenced by sporadic contacts with traders, they went on to iron and, by now, a primitive combustion-powered technology which was spreading their hegemony across the world. The process was slower than it had been on Terra; Shalmuans were less ferocious, less able to treat their fellow beings like vermin or machinery, than humankind is.

They were happy to come under the Empire. It meant protection from barbarian starfarers, who had already caused them grief. They did not see the Naval base they got. It was elsewhere in the system. Why risk a living planet, if matters came to a local fight, when a barren one served equally well? But there was a small marine garrison on Shalmu, and spacemen visited it on leave, and this attracted a scattering of Imperial civilians, who traded with the autochthons as readily as with service personnel. Shalmuans found employment among these foreigners. A few got to go outsystem. A smaller but growing number were recommended for scholarships by Terran friends, and returned with modern educations. The dream grew of entering civilization as a full-fledged member.

In return, Shalmu paid modest taxes in kind: metals, fuels, foodstuffs, saleable works of art and similar luxuries, depending on what a particular area could furnish. It accepted an Imperial resident, whose word was the ultimate law but who in practice let native cultures fairly well alone. His marines did suppress wars and banditry as far as practicable, but this was considered good by most. The young Imperials, human or nonhuman, often conducted themselves arrogantly, but whatever serious harm they might inflict on an innocent Shalmuan resulted, as a rule, in punishment.

In short, the planet was typical of the majority that had fallen under Terran sway. Backward, they had more to gain than lose; they saw mainly the bright side of the Imperial coin, which was not too badly tarnished.

Or so the case had been till a couple of years ago.

Flandry stood on a hill. Behind him were five men, bodyguards from his crew. Beside him was Ch'kessa, Prime in Council of the Clan Towns of Att. Ch'kessa's home community sprawled down the slope, a collection of neat, whitewashed, drum-shaped houses where several thousand individuals lived. Though peaked, each sod roof was a flower garden, riotous with color. The ways between houses were "paved" with a tough mossy growth, except where fruit trees grew from which anyone might help himself when they bore and no one took excessively. Pastures and cultivated fields occupied the valley beneath. On its other side, the hills were wooded.

Apart from somewhat weaker gravity, Shalmu was terrestroid. Every detail might be strange, but the overall effect spoke to ancient human instincts. Broad plains, tall moun-

24

tains, spindrift across unrestful seas; rustling sun-flecked shadows in a forest, unexpected sweetness of tiny white blossoms between old roots; the pride of a great horned beast, the lonesome cries descending from migratory wings; and the people. Ch'kessa's features were not so different from Flandry's. Hairless bright-green skin, prehensile tail, 140-centimeter height, details of face, foot, hand, interior anatomy, exoticism of his embroidered wraparound and plumed spirit wand and other accouterments—did they matter?

The wind shifted. On planets like this, the air had always seemed purer than anywhere on Terra, be it in the middle of a nobleman's enormous private park. Away from machines, you drew more life into your lungs. But Flandry gagged. One of his men must suddenly vomit.

"That is why we obeyed the new resident," Ch'kessa said. He spoke fluent Anglic.

Down the hill, lining a valleyward road, ran a hundred wooden crosses. The bodies lashed to them had not finished rotting. Carrion birds and insects still made black clouds around them, under a wantonly brilliant summer sky.

"Do you see?" Ch'kessa asked anxiously. "We did refuse at first. Not the heavy taxes the new resident laid on us. I am told he did that throughout the world. He said it was to pay for meeting a terrible danger. He did not say what the danger was. However, we paid, especially after we heard how bombs were dropped or soldiers came with torches where folk protested. I do not think the old resident would have done that. Nor do I think the Emperor, may his name echo in eternity, would let those things happen if he knew."

Actually, Flandry did not answer, *Josip wouldn't give a damn. Or maybe he would. Maybe he'd ask to see films of the action, and watch them and giggle.* The wind changed again, and he blessed it for taking away part of the charnel odor.

"We paid," Ch'kessa said. "That was not easy, but we remember the barbarians too well. Then this season a fresh demand was put before us. We, who had powder rifles, were to supply males. They would be flown to lands like Yanduvar, where folk lack firearms. There they would catch natives for the slave market. I do not understand, though I have often asked. Why does the Empire, with many machines, need slaves?"

Personal service, Flandry did not answer. *For instance, the sort women supply. We use enslavement as one kind of criminal penalty. But it isn't too significant. There isn't that big a percentage of slaves in the Empire. The barbarians, though, would pay well for skilled hands. And transactions with them do not get into any Imperial records for some officious computer to come upon at a later date.*

"Continue," he said aloud.

"The Council of the Clan Towns of Att debated long," Ch'kessa said. "We were afraid. Still, the thing was not right for us to do. At length we decided to make excuses, to delay as much as might be, while messengers sped overland to Iscoyn. There the Imperial marine base is, as my lord well knows. The messengers would appeal to the commandant, that he intercede for us with the resident."

Flandry caught a mutter behind him: "Nova flash! Is he saying the marines hadn't been enforcing the decrees?"

"Yeh, sure," growled an adjacent throat. "Forget your barroom brawls with 'em. They wouldn't commit vileness like this. Mercenaries did it. Now dog your hatch before the Old Man hears you."

Me? Flandry thought in stupid astonishment. *Me, the Old Man?*

"I suppose our messengers were caught and their story twisted from them," Ch'kessa sighed. "At least, they never returned. A legate came and told us we must obey. We refused. Troops came. They herded us together. A hundred were chosen by lot and put on the crosses. The rest of us had to watch till all were dead. It took three days and nights. One of my daughters was among them." He pointed. His arm was not steady. "Perhaps my lord can see her. That quite small body, eleventh on our left. It is black and swollen, and much of it has fallen off, but she used to come stumping and laughing to meet me when I returned from work. She cried for me to help her. The cries were many, yet I heard hers. Whenever I moved toward her, a shock beam stopped me. I had not thought there could be happiness in seeing her die. We were instructed to leave the bodies in place, on pain of bombing. An aircraft flies over from time to time to make sure."

He sat down in the whispering silvery pseudograss, put face on knees and tail across neck. His fingers plucked at the dirt. "After that," he said, "we went slaving."

Flandry stood silent for a space. He had been furious at the carnage being inflicted by the more advanced Shalmuans on the weaker ones. Swooping down on a caravan of chained prisoners, he had arrested its leader and demanded an explanation. Ch'kessa had suggested they flit to his homeland.

"Where are your villagers?" Flandry asked at length, for the houses stood empty, smokeless, silent.

26

"They cannot live here with those dead," Ch'kessa replied. "They camp out, coming back only to maintain. And doubtless they fled when they saw your boat, my lord, not knowing what you would do." He looked up. "You have seen. Are we deeply to blame? Will you return me to my gang? A sum is promised each of us for each slave we bring in. It is helpful in meeting the tax. I will not get mine if I am absent when the caravan reaches the airfield."

"Yes." Flandry turned. His cloak swirled behind him. "Let's go."

Another low voice at his back: "I never swallowed any brotherhood-of-beings crap, you know that, Sam'l, but when our own xenos are scared by a vessel of ours—!"

"Silence," Flandry ordered.

The gig lifted with a yell and trailed a thunderbolt across half a continent and an ocean. Nobody spoke. When she tilted her nose toward jungle, Ch'kessa ventured to say, "Perhaps you will intercede for us, my lord."

"I'll do my best," Flandry said.

"When the Emperor hears, let him not be angry with us of the Clan Towns. We went unwillingly. We sicken with fevers and die from the poisoned arrows of the Yanduvar folk."

And wreck what was a rather promising culture, Flandry thought.

"If punishment must be for what we have done, let it fall on me alone," Ch'kessa begged. "That does not matter greatly after I watched my little one die."

"Be patient," Flandry said. "The Emperor has many peoples who need his attention. Your turn will come."

Inertial navigation had pinpointed the caravan, and a mere couple of hours had passed since. Flandry's pilot soon found it, trudging down a swale where ambush was less likely than among trees. He landed the gig a kilometer off and opened the airlock.

"Farewell, my lord." The Shalmuan knelt, coiled his tail around Flandry's ankles, crawled out and was gone. His slim green form bounded toward his kin.

"Return to the ship," Flandry instructed.

"Doesn't the captain wish to pay a courtesy call on the resident?" asked the pilot sarcastically. He was not long out of the Academy. His hue remained sick.

"Get aloft, Citizen Willig," Flandry said. "You know we're on an information-gathering mission and in a hurry. We didn't notify anyone except Navy that we'd been on Starport or New Indra, did we?"

The ensign sent hands dancing across the board. The gig

stood on its tail with a violence that would have thrown everybody into the stern were it not for acceleration compensators. "Excuse me, sir," he said between his teeth. "A question, if the captain pleases. Haven't we witnessed outright illegality? I mean, those other two planets were having a bad time, but nothing like this. Because the Shalmuans have no way to get a complaint off their world, I suppose. Isn't our duty, sir, to report what we've seen?"

Sweat glistened on his forehead and stained his tunic beneath the arms. Flandry caught an acrid whiff of it. Glancing about, he saw the other four men leaning close, straining to hear through the throb of power and whistle of cloven atmosphere. *Should I answer?* he asked himself, a touch frantically. *And if so, what can I tell him that won't be bad for discipline? How should I know? I'm too young to be the Old Man!*

He gained time with a cigaret. Stars trod forth in viewscreens as the gig entered space. Willig exchanged a signal with the ship, set the controls for homing on her, and swiveled around to join in staring at his captain.

Flandry sucked in smoke, trickled it out, and said cautiously: "You have been told often enough, we are first on a fact-finding mission, second at the disposal of Alpha Crucis Command if we can help without prejudice to the primary assignment. Whatever we learn will be duly reported. If any man wishes to file additional material or comment, that's his privilege. However, you should be warned that it isn't likely to go far. And this is not because inconvenient facts will be swept under the carpet, *though I daresay that does happen on occasion.* "It's due to the overwhelming volume of data."

He gestured. "A hundred thousand planets, gentlemen, more or less," he said. "Each with its millions or billions of inhabitants, its complexities and mysteries, its geographies. and civilizations, their pasts and presents and conflicting aims for the future, therefore each with its own complicated, ever-changing, unique set of relationships to the Imperium. We can't control that, can we? We can't even hope to comprehend it. At most, we can try to maintain the Pax. At most, gentlemen.

"What's right in one place may be wrong in another. One species may be combative and anarchic by nature, another peaceful and antlike, a third peaceful and anarchic, a fourth a bunch of aggressive totalitarian hives. I know a planet where murder and cannibalism are necessary to race survival: high radiation background, you see, making for high mutation rate coupled with chronic food shortage. The unfit must

28

be eaten. I know of intelligent hermaphrodites, and sophonts with more than two sexes, and a few that regularly change sex. They all tend to look on our reproductive pattern as obscene. I could go on for hours. Not to mention the variations imposed by culture. Just think about Terran history.

"And then the sheer number of individuals and interests; the sheer distance; the time needed to get a message across our territory— No, we can't direct everything. We haven't the manpower. And if we did, it'd remain physically impossible to coordinate that many data.

"We've *got* to give our proconsuls wide discretion. We've *got* to let them recruit auxiliaries, and hope those auxiliaries will know the local scene better than Imperial regulars. Above all, gentlemen, for survival if nothing else, we've *got* to preserve solidarity."

He waved a hand at the forward viewscreen. Alpha Crucis blazed lurid among the constellations; but beyond it— "If we don't stick together, we Terrans and our nonhuman allies," he said, "I assure you, either the Merseians or the wild races will be delighted to stick us separately."

He got no reply: not that he expected one. *Was that a sufficiently stuffy speech?* he wondered.

And was it sufficiently truthful?

I don't know about that last. Nor do I know if I have any right to inquire.

His ship swam into sight. The tiny spindle, well-nigh lost beside the vast glowing bulk of the planet she circled, grew to a steel barracuda, guns rakish across the star clouds. She was no more than an escort destroyer, she had speed but was lightly armed, her crew numbered a bare fifty. Nevertheless, she was Flandry's first official command and his blood ran a little faster each time he saw her—even now, even now.

The gig made a ragged approach. Willig probably didn't feel well yet. Flandry refrained from commenting. The last part of the curve, under computer choreography, was better. When the boat housing had closed and repressurized, he dismissed his guards and went alone to the bridge.

Halls, companionways, and shafts were narrow. They were painted gray and white. With the interior grav generators set for full Terran weight, thin deckplates resounded under boots, thin bulkheads cast the noise back and forth, voices rang, machinery droned and thumped. The air that gusted from ventilator grilles came fresh out of the renewers, but somehow it collected a faint smell of oil on the way. The officers' cabins were cubbyholes, the forecastle could be packed tighter only if the Pauli exclusion principle were repealed, the

29

recreation facilities were valuable chiefly as a subject for jokes, and the less said about the galley the wiser. But she was Flandry's first command.

He had spent many hours en route reading her official history and playing back tapes of former logbooks. She was a few years older than him. Her name derived from a land mass on Ardèche, which was apparently a human-settled planet though not one he had ever chanced upon mention of. (He knew the designation Asieneuve in different versions on at least four worlds; and he speculated on how many other Continent-class vessels bore it. A name was a mere flourish when computers must deal with millions of craft by their numbers.) She had gone on occasional troopship convoy when trouble broke loose on a surface somewhere. Once she had been engaged in a border incident; her captain claimed a probably hit but lacked adequate proof. Otherwise her existence had been routine patrols . . . which were essential, were they not?

You didn't salute under these conditions. Men squeezed themselves aside to make way for Flandry. He entered the bridge. His executive officer had it.

Rovian of Ferra was slightly more than human size. His fur was velvet at midnight. His ponderous tail, the claws on his feet and fingers, the saber teeth in his jaws, could deal murderous blows; he was also an expert marksman. The lower pair of his four arms could assist his legs at need. Then his silent undulant gait turned into lightning. He habitually went nude except for guns and insignia. His nature and nurture were such that he would never become a captain and did not want to be. But he was capable and well liked, and Terran citizenship had been conferred on him.

"S-s-so?" he greeted. His fangs handicapped him a little in speaking Anglic.

Alone, he and Flandry didn't bother to be formal. Mankind's rituals amused him. "Bad," the master said, and explained.

"Why bad?" Rovian asked. "Unless it provokes revolt."

"Never mind the morals of it. You wouldn't understand. Consider the implications, however."

Flandry inhaled a cigaret to lighting. His gaze sought Shalmu's disc, where it floated unutterably peaceful in its day and night. "Why should Snelund do this?" he said. "It's considerable trouble, and not without hazard. Ordinary corruption would earn him more than he could live to spend on himself. He must have a larger purpose, one that requires moonsful of money. What is it?"

30

Rovian erected the chemosensor antennae that flanked the bony ridge on his skull. His muzzle twitched, his eyes glowed yellow. "To finance an insurrection? He may hope to become an independent overlord."

"M-m-m . . . no . . . doesn't make sense, and I gather he's not stupid. The Empire can't conceivably tolerate breakaways. He'd have to be crushed. If necessary, Josip would be deposed to clear the track for that operation. No, something else—" Flandry brought his attention back. "Get patrol clearance for us to go in half an hour. Next rendezvous, Llynathawr."

Hyperdrive vibrations are instantaneous, though the philosophers of science have never agreed on the meaning of that adjective. Unfortunately, they damp out fast. No matter how powerful, a signal cannot be received beyond a distance of about one light-year. Thus spaceships traveling at quasivelocity are not detectable by their "wakes" at any farther remove than that. Neither are the modulations that carry messages quicker than light; and the uncertainty principle makes it impossible to relay them with any hope that they will not soon degenerate into gibberish.

Accordingly, *Asieneuve* was within two hours of her goal before she got the news. Fleet Admiral Hugh McCormac had escaped to the Virgilian System. There he had raised the standard of rebellion and proclaimed himself Emperor. An unspecified number of planets had declared for him. So had an unspecified proportion of the ships and men he formerly commanded. Armed clashes had taken place and full civil war looked inevitable.

IV

~~~~~~~~~

When the Empire purchased Llynathawr from its Cynthian discoverers, the aim had been to strengthen this frontier by attracting settlers. Most of the world was delightful in climate and scenery, rich in natural resources, wide in unclaimed lands. Navy sector headquarters were close enough, on Ifri, and housed enough power to give ample protection. Not all the barbarians were hostile; there existed excellent possibilities of trade with a number of races—especially those that had not acquired spacecraft—as well as with Imperial planets.

Thus far the theory. Three or four generations showed that practice was something else again. The human species appeared to have lost its outward urge. Few individuals would leave a familiar, not too uncomfortable environment to start over in a place remote from government-guaranteed security and up-to-date entertainment. Those who did usually preferred city to rural life. Nor did many arrive from the older colonies nearby, like Aeneas. Such people had struck their own roots.

Catawrayannis did become a substantial town: two million, if you counted in the floating population. It became the seat of the civil authority. It became a brisk mart, though much of the enterprise was carried on by nonhumans, and a pleasure resort, and a regional listening post. But that was the end of the process. The hinterland, latifundia, mines, factories, soon gave way to forests, mountains, trafficless oceans, empty plains, a wilderness where lights gleamed rare and lonely after dark.

Of course, this has the advantage of not turning the planet as a whole into still another cesspool, Flandry thought. After reporting, he had donned mufti and spent a few days incognito. Besides sounding out various bourgeoisie and servants, he had passed through a particularly ripe Lowtown.

And now I feel so respectable I creak, his mind went on. *Contrast? No, not when I'm about to meet Aaron Snelund.* His pulse quickened. He must make an effort to keep his face and bearing expressionless. That skill he owed less to official training than to hundreds of poker games.

As a ramp lifted him toward an impressive portico, he glanced back. The gubernatorial palace crowned a high hill. It was a big pastel-tinted structure in the dome-and-colonnade style of the last century. Beneath its gardens, utilitarian office buildings for civil servants made terraces to the flatland. Homes of the wealthy ringed the hill. Beyond these, more modest residences blended gradually into cropground on the west side, city on the east. Commercial towers, none very tall, clustered near the Luana River, past which lay the slums. A haze blurred vision today and the breeze blew cool, tasting of spring. Vehicles moved insectlike through streets and sky. Their sound came as a whisper, almost hidden in the sough of trees. It was hard to grasp that Catawrayannis brawled with preparation for war, shrilled with hysteria, tensed with fear—

—until a slow thundering went from horizon to horizon, and a spatial warcraft crossed heaven on an unknown errand.

Two marines flanked the main entrance. "Please state your name and business, sir," one demanded. He didn't aim his slug-thrower, but his knuckles stood white on butt and barrel.

"Commander Dominic Flandry, captain, HMS *Asieneuve*, here for an appointment with His Excellency."

"A moment, please." The other marine checked. He didn't merely call the secretarial office, he turned a scanner on the newcomer. "All right."

"If you'll leave your sidearm with me, sir," the first man said. "And, uh, submit to a brief search."

"Hey?" Flandry blinked.

"Governor's orders, sir. Nobody who doesn't have a special pass with full physical ID goes through armed or unchecked." The marine, who was pathetically young, wet his lips. "You understand, sir. When Navy units commit treason, we . . . who dare we trust?"

Flandry looked into the demoralized countenance, surrendered his blaster, and allowed hands to feel across his whites.

A servant appeared, bowed, and escorted him down a corridor and up a gravshaft. The décor was luxurious, its bad taste more a question of subtly too much opulence than of garish colors or ugly proportions. The same applied to the chamber where Flandry was admitted. A live-fur carpet reached gold and black underfoot; iridescences swept over the walls; dynasculps moved in every corner; incense and low music tinged the air; instead of an exterior view, an animation of an Imperial court masquerade occupied one entire side; behind the governor's chair of state hung a thrice life-size, thrice flattering portrait of Emperor Josip, fulsomely inscribed.

Four mercenaries were on guard, not human but giant shaggy Gorzunians. They stirred scarcely more than their helmets, breastplates, or weapons.

Flandry saluted and stood at attention.

Snelund did not look diabolical. He had bought himself an almost girlish beauty: flame-red wavy hair, creamy skin, slightly slanted violet eyes, retroussé nose, bee-stung lips. Though not tall, and now growing paunchy, he retained some of his dancer's gracefulness. His richly patterned tunic, flare-cut trousers, petal-shaped shoes, and gold necklace made Flandry envious.

Rings sparkled as he turned a knob on a memoscreen built into the chair arm. "Ah, yes. Good day, Commander." His voice was pleasant. "I can give you fifteen minutes." He smiled. "My apologies for such curtness, and for your having to wait this long to see me. You can guess how hectic things are. If Admiral Pickens had not informed me you come directly from Intelligence HQ, I'm afraid you'd never have gotten past my office staff." He chuckled. "Sometimes I think they're overzealous about protecting me. One does appreciate their fending off as many bores and triviators as possible—though you'd be surprised, Commander, how many I cannot escape seeing—but occasionally, no doubt, undue delay is caused a person with a valid problem."

"Yes, Your Excellency. Not to waste your time—"

"Do sit down. It's good to meet someone straight from the Mother of us all. We don't even get frequent mail out here, you know. How fares old Terra?"

"Well, Your Excellency, I was only there a few days, and quite busy most of them." Flandry seated himself and leaned forward. "About my assignment."

"Of course, of course," Snelund said. "But grant me a moment first." His geniality was replaced by an appearance of concern. His tone sharpened. "Have you fresh news of the Merseian situation? We're as worried about that as anyone in the Empire, despite our own current difficulties. Perhaps more worried than most. Transfer of units to that border has

34

gravely weakened this. Let war break out with Merseia, and we could be depleted still further—an invitation to the barbarians. That's why McCormac's rebellion must be suppressed immediately, no matter the cost."

Flandry realized: *I'm being stalled.* "I know nothing that isn't public, sir," he said at a leisured rate. "I'm sure Ifri HQ gets regular couriers from the Betelgeusean marches. The information gap is in the other direction, if I may use a metaphor which implies that gaps aren't isotropic."

Snelund laughed. "Well spoken, Commander. One grows starved for a little wit. Frontiers are traditionally energetic but unimaginative."

"Thank you, Your Excellency," Flandry said. "I'd better state my business, though. Will the governor bear with me if I sound long-winded? Necessary background . . . especially since my assignment is indefinite, really just to prepare a report on whatever I can learn. . . ."

Snelund lounged back. "Proceed."

"As a stranger to these parts," Flandry said pompously, "I had to begin with studying references and questioning a broad spectrum of people. My application for an interview with you, sir, would have been cancelled had it turned out to be needless. For I do see how busy you are in this crisis. As matters developed, however, I found I'd have to make a request of you. A simple thing, fortunately. You need only issue an order."

"Well?" Snelund invited.

He's relaxed now, Flandry judged: *takes me for the usual self-important favorite nephew, going through a charade to furnish an excuse for my next promotion.*

"I would like to interview the Lady McCormac," he said.

Snelund jerked upright where he sat.

"My information is that she was arrested together with her husband and has been detained in Your Excellency's personal custody," Flandry said with a fatuous smile. "I'm sure she has a good many valuable data. And I've speculated about using her as a go-between. A negotiated settlement with her husband—"

"No negotiation with a traitor!" Snelund's fist smote a chair arm.

How dramatic, Flandry thought. Aloud: "Pardon me, sir. I didn't mean he should get off scot free, simply that—Well, anyhow, I was surprised to discover no one has questioned the Lady McCormac."

Snelund said indignantly, "I know what you've heard. They gossip around here like a gaggle of dirty-minded old women.

35

I've explained the facts to Admiral Pickens' chief Intelligence officer, and I'll explain them again to you. She appears to have an unstable personality, worse even than her husband's. Their arrest threw her into a completely hysterical condition. Or 'psychotic' might not be too strong a word. As a humane gesture, I put her in a private room rather than a cell. There was less evidence against her than him. She's quartered in my residential wing because that's the sole place where I can guarantee her freedom from bumbling interruptions. My agents were preparing to quiz McCormac in depth when his fellow criminals freed him. His wife heard, and promptly attempted suicide. My medical staff has had to keep her under heavy sedation ever since."

Flandry had been told otherwise, though no one dared give him more than hearsay. "I beg the governor's pardon," he said. "The admiral's staff suggested perhaps I, with a direct assignment, might be allowed where they aren't."

"Their men have met her twice, Commander. In neither case was she able to testify."

No, it isn't hard to give a prisoner a shot or a touch of brainshock, when you have an hour or two advance notice. "I see, Your Excellency. And she hasn't improved?"

"She's worsened. On medical advice, I've banned further visits. What could the poor woman relate, anyway?"

"Probably nothing, Your Excellency. However, you'll appreciate, sir, I'm supposed to make a full report. And as my ship will soon be leaving with the fleet," *unless I produce my authority to detach her,* "this may be my lone chance. Couldn't I have a few minutes, to satisfy them on Terra?"

Snelund bristled. "Do you doubt my word, Commander?"

"Oh, no, Your Excellency! Never! This is strictly *pro forma.* To save my, uh, reputation, sir, because they'll ask why I didn't check this detail also. I could go there straight from here, sir, and your medics could be on hand to keep me from doing any harm."

Snelund shook his head. "I happen to know you would. I forbid it."

Flandry gave him a reproachful stare.

Snelund tugged his chin. "Of course, I sympathize with your position," he said, trading a scowl for a slight smile. "Terra is so far away that our reality can only come through as words, photographs, charts. Um-m-m. . . . Give me a number where you can be contacted on short notice. I'll have my chief doctor inform you when you can go to her. Some days she's more nearly sane than others, though at best she's incoherent. Will that do?"

"Your Excellency is most kind," Flandry beamed.

"I don't promise she'll be available before you depart," Snelund cautioned. "Small time remains. If not, you can doubtless see her on your return. Though that will hardly be worth the trouble, will it, after McCormac has been put down?"

Pro forma, Your Excellency," Flandry repeated.

The governor recorded a memorandum, including a phone exchange which would buck a message on to *Asieneuve,* and Flandry took his leave with expressions of mutual esteem.

He got a cab outside the palace and made sure he was heard directing it to the shuttleport. It was no secret that he'd been on the ground these past several days; his job required that. But the fainéant impression he wanted to give would be reinforced if he took the first excuse to return to his vessel. Ascetical though his cabin there might be, it was a considerable improvement on the flea circus dormitory which was the best planetside quarters a late arrival like him had been able to obtain. Catawrayannis was overflowing at the hatches with spacemen and marines, as ship after ship made rendezvous.

"Why here?" he had asked Captain Leclerc, the member of Admiral Pickens' staff to whom he actually reported. "Ifri is HQ."

Leclerc shrugged. "The governor wants it this way."

"But he can't—"

"He can, Flandry. I know, the Naval and civilian provincial commands are supposed to be coordinate. But the governor is the Emperor's direct representative. As such, he can invoke Imperial authority when he wants. It may get him into the kettle on Terra afterward, but that's afterward. On the spot, the Navy had better heed him."

"Why the order, though? Ifri has the main facilities. It's our natural center and starting point."

"Well, yes, but Llynathawr doesn't have Ifri's defenses. By our presence, we guard against any revengeful raids McCormac may plan. It makes a degree of sense, even. Knocking out the sector capital—or preferably occupying it—would put him a long way toward control of the entire region. Once we get started, he'll be too busy with us to think about that, although naturally we will leave some protection." Leclerc added cynically: "While they wait, our men on liberty will enjoy a good, expensive last fling. Snelund's careful to stay popular in Catawrayannis."

"Do you really think we should charge out for an immediate full-dress battle?"

"Governor's directive again, I hear. It certainly doesn't fit

37

Admiral Pickens' temperament. Left alone, I'm convinced he'd see what could be done first by dickering and small-scale shooting . . . rather than maybe end up bombarding Imperial worlds into radioactive rubbish. But the word is, we've got to blast the infection before it spreads." Leclerc grimaced. "You're an insidious one. I've no business talking like this. Let's take up your business!"

—When he stepped out at the terminal, Flandry received the not unexpected information that he must wait a couple of hours for a seat on a ferry to Satellite Eight, where he could summon his gig. He phoned the dormitory and had his luggage shunted to him. Since this consisted merely of one handbag, already packed, he didn't bother to check it, but carried it along into a refresher booth. From there he emerged in drab civvies, with a hooded cloak and slouching gait and bag turned inside out to show a different color. He had no real reason to think he had been followed, but he believed in buying insurance when it was cheap. He took a cab to an unpretentious hotel, thence another into Lowtown. The last few blocks he walked.

Rovian had found a rooming house whose clientele were mostly nonhumans: unchoosy ones. He shared his kennel with a betentacled hulk from an unpronounceable planet. The hulk reeked of exuded hydrogen sulfide but was personally decent enough; among other sterling qualities, it did not know the Eriau language. It rippled on its bunk when Flandry entered, mushed an Anglic greeting, and returned to contemplation of whatever it contemplated.

Rovian stretched all six limbs and yawned alarmingly. "At last!" he said. "I thought I would rot."

Flandry sat down on the floor, which carried no chairs, and lit a cigaret more against the stench than because he wanted one. "How goes the ship?" he asked in the principal Merseian tongue.

"Satisfactorily," Rovian answered likewise. "Some were curious at the exec absenting himself before the captain returned. But I passed it off as needful to our supplying and left Valencia in charge. Nothing can really happen while we idle in orbit, so no great comment followed."

Flandry met the slit-pupilled eyes. *You seem to know more about what your human shipmates think than a xeno should,* he did not say. *I don't pretend to understand what goes on in your brain. But . . . I have to rely on somebody. Sounding you out while we traveled, as well as might be, I decided you're least improbably the one.*

"I didn't ask you to locate a den, and tell me where, and

38

wait, for sport," he declared with the explicitness required by Eriau grammar. "My idea was that we'd need privacy for laying plans. That's been confirmed."

Rovian cocked his ears.

Flandry described his session with the governor. He finished: "No reasonable doubt remains that Snelund is lying about Lady McCormac's condition. Gossip leaks through guards and servants, out of the private apartments and into the rest of the palace. Nobody cares, aside from malicious amusement. He's packed the court, like the housecarls and the residencies, with his own creatures. Snooping around, getting sociable with people off duty, I led them to talk. Two or three of them got intoxicated till they said more than they would have normally." He didn't mention the additives he had slipped into their drinks.

"Why don't the regular Intelligence officers suspect?" Rovian inquired.

"Oh, I imagine they do. But they have so much else to deal with, so obviously vital. And they don't think she can tell anything useful. And why collide with the governor, risking your career, for the sake of the arch-rebel's wife?"

"You wish to," Rovian pounced.

"*Kraich.*" Flandry squinted into the smoke he was blowing. It curled blue-gray across what sunlight straggled through a window whose grime seemed of geologic age. The rotten-egg gas was giving him a headache, unless that was due to the general odor of decay. Faintly from outside came traffic rumble and an occasional raucous cry.

"You see," he explained, "I'm on detached service. My nose isn't committed to any of the numberless grindstones which must be turned before a Naval expedition can get under way. And I have more background on Aaron Snelund than provincial officers do, even in my own corps and in his own preserve. I've been free and able to sit and wonder. And I decided it wasn't logical he should keep Kathryn McCormac locked away simply for the purpose the court is sniggering about. The admiral's staff may think so, and not care. But I doubt if he's capable of feeling more than a passing attraction for any fellow creature. Why not turn her over for interrogation? She might know a little something after all. Or she might be handy in dealing with her husband."

"Scarcely that," Rovian said. "His life is already forfeit."

"Uh-huh. Which is why my harried colleagues didn't check further. But—oh, I can't predict—her, in exchange for various limited concessions on his part—her, persuading him to give up—Well, I suppose it takes a cold-blooded bastard like me to consider such possibilities. The point is, we can't lose by trying her out, and might gain a trifle. Therefore we ought to. But Snelund is holding her back with a yarn about her illness. Why? What's in it for him, besides herself? His sector's being torn apart. Why isn't he more cooperative in this tiny matter?"

"I couldn't say." Rovian implied indifference.

"I wonder if she may not know something he would prefer didn't get out," Flandry said. "The assumption has been that Snelund may be a bad governor, but he is loyal and Mc-Cormac's the enemy. It's only an assumption."

"Should you not then invoke the authority in your second set of orders, and demand her person?"

Flandry made a face. "Huh! Give them five minutes of stalling at the gate, and I'll be presented with a corpse. Or ten minutes under a misused hypnoprobe could produce a memoryless idiot. Wherefore I walked very softly indeed. I don't expect to be summoned before the fleet leaves, either."

"And on our return—"

"She can easily have 'passed away' during the campaign."

Rovian tautened. The bunk where he crouched made a groaning noise. "You tell me this for a purpose, captain," he said.

Flandry nodded. "How did you guess?"

Again Rovian waited, until the man sighed and proceeded:

"I think we can spring her loose, if we time it exactly right. You'll be here in town, with some crewmen you've picked and an aircar handy. An hour or so before the armada accelerates, I'll present my sealed orders to the admiral and formally remove us from his command. It's a safe bet Snelund's attention will be on the fleet, not on the palace. You'll take your squad there, serve a warrant I'll have given you, and collect Kathryn McCormac before anybody can raise the governor and ask what to do. If need be, you can shoot; whoever tries to stop you will be in defiance of the Imperium. But I doubt the necessity will arise if you work fast. I'll have the gig waiting not too far off. You and your lads flit Lady McCormac there, haul gravs for space, rendezvous with *Asieneuve*, and we'll depart this system in a hurry."

"The scheme appears hazardous," Rovian said, "and for slight probable gain."

"It's all I can think of," Flandry answered. "I know you'll be getting the operative end of the reamer. Refuse if you think I'm a fool."

Rovian licked his saber teeth and switched his tail. "I do

not refuse my captain," he said, "I, a Brother of the Oath. It does seem to me that we might discuss the problem further. I believe your tactics could be made somewhat more elegant."

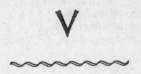

V

Ship by ship, Pickens' forces departed orbit and moved outward. When the sun of Llynathawr had shrunk to a bright point, the vessels assumed formation and went into hyperdrive. Space swirled with impalpable energies. As one, the warcraft and their ministrants aimed themselves at the star called Virgil, to find the man who would be Emperor.

They were not many. Reassignments, to help confront Merseia, had depleted the sector fleet. A shocking number of units had subsequently joined McCormac. Of those which stayed true, enough must remain behind to screen—if not solidly guard—the key planets. It was estimated that the rebels had about three-fourths the strength that Pickens would be able to bring to bear on them. Given nuclear-headed missiles and firebeams powered by hydrogen fusion, such numerical comparisons are less meaningful than the layman thinks. A single penetration of defenses can put a ship out of action, often out of existence.

On that account, Pickens traveled cautiously, inside a wide-flung net of scoutboats. His fastest vessels could have covered the distance in a day and a half, his slowest in twice that time; but he planned on a whole five days. He had not forgotten the trap his former commander sprang on the Valdotharian corsairs.

And on the bridge of *Asieneuve*, Dominic Flandry leaned forward in his control chair and said: "Twenty degrees north, four degrees clockwise, 3000 kilometers negative, then match quasi-velocities and steady as she goes."

"Aye, sir." The pilot repeated the instructions and programmed the computer that operated the hyperdrive.

Flandry kept his attention on the console before him, whose meters and readouts summarized the far more complex data with which the pilot dealt, until he dared say, "Can you hold this course, Citizen Rovian?"

In point of fact, he was asking his executive officer if the destroyer was moving as planned—tagging along after the fleet in order that her wake be drowned in many and that she thus be hidden from pursuit. They both knew, and both knew the master's ritual infallibility must be preserved. Rovian studied the board and said, "Aye, sir," with complete solemnity.

Flandry opened the general intercom. "Now hear this," he intoned. "Captain to all officers and crew. You are aware that our ship has a special mission, highly confidential and of the utmost importance. We are finally embarked on it. For success, we require absolute communications silence. No messages will be received except by Lieutenant Commander Rovian or myself, nor will any be sent without my express authorization. When treason has infected His Majesty's very Navy, the danger of subversion and of ruses must be guarded against." *How's that for casuistry?* he grinned within. "The communications officer will set his circuits accordingly. Carry on."

He switched off. His gaze lifted to the simulacrum of heaven projected on the viewscreens. No spacecraft showed. The greatest of them was lost in immensity, findable only by instruments and esoteric calculations. The stars ignored them, were not touched by the wars and pains of life, were immortal—*No, not that either. They have their own Long Night waiting for them.*

"Outercom circuits ready, sir," Rovian announced after a study of the main panel. He slipped on a headband receiver. Every incoming signal would go there, to be heard by him alone.

"Take the bridge, then." Flandry rose. "I'll interrogate the prisoner. When the time comes to change vectors, notify me immediately but don't wait for me to arrive before you do it."

What he really told Rovian was: Monitor transmissions. Snelund's bound to yell when he learns what's happened. If we're out of hyperwave range by that time, he'll probably send a boat after us. Either way, he'll demand our return, and Pickens might well give in. That could make a delicate situation. The minute it looks like coming about, we're to

42

sheer off and get the devil away. I'd rather be able to prove by the log that I never could have received any order from Pickens, than try to make a court-martial agree I was right in disregarding it.

But those two alone knew the code. Possibly the ratings who had gone to the palace with their exec could have guessed. No matter there. They were tough and close-mouthed and, after what they had seen en route from Terra, callously cheerful about any inconvenience they might have caused His Excellency.

"Aye, sir," said Rovian.

Flandry went down a companionway and along a throbbing passage to his cabin. The door had no chime. He knocked.

"Who is it?" The voice that came through the thin panel was a husky contralto, singingly accented—and how tired, how empty!

"Captain, my lady. May I come in?"

"I can't stop you."

Flandry stepped through and closed the door behind him. His cabin had room for little more than a bunk, a desk and chair, a closet, some shelves and drawers. His bonnet brushed the overhead. A curtain hid a washbasin, toilet, and shower stall. He'd had no chance to install many personal possessions. The sound and vibration and oily-electrical odor of the ship filled the air.

He had not even seen a picture of Kathryn McCormac. Suddenly everything else dissolved around him. He thought afterward he must have given her a courtly bow, because he found his bonnet clutched in his fingers, but he couldn't remember.

She was five standard years older than him, he knew, and in no Terran fashion of beauty. Her figure was too tall, too wide-shouldered and deep-bosomed, too firmly muscled beneath a skin that was still, after her imprisonment, too sun-tanned. The face was broad: across the high cheekbones, between the luminous eyes (gold-flecked green under thick black brows), in the blunt nose and generous mouth and strong chin. Her hair was banged over her forehead, bobbed below her ears, thick and wavy, amber with shadings of gold and copper. She wore the brief nacreous gown and crystaflex sandals in which she had been taken from the palace.

Mother looked sort of like her, Flandry realized.

He hauled his wits back in. "Welcome aboard, my lady." He could feel his smile was a touch unstable. "Permit me to

43

introduce myself." He did. "Entirely at your service," he finished, and held out his hand.

She did not give him hers, either to shake or kiss, nor did she rise from his chair. He observed the darknesses around and behind her eyes, hollowing of cheeks, faint dusting of freckles. . . . "Good day, Commander." Her tone was not warm or cold or anything.

Flandry lowered his bunk and himself onto it. "What may I offer you?" he asked. "We have the regular assortment of drinks and drugs. And would you like a bite to eat?" He extended his opened cigaret case.

"Nothin'."

He regarded her. *Stop skyhooting, son. You've been celibate unrightfully long. She's handsome and*—he dragged it forth—*no doubt you speculated about her possible availability . . . after what's happened to her. Forget it. Save your villainies for the opposition.*

He said slowly: "You don't want to accept hospitality from the Imperium. Correct? Please be sensible, my lady. You know you'll take nourishment to stay alive, as you did in Snelund's house. Why not begin now? My cause isn't necessarily irreconcilable with yours. I had you fetched here, at some risk, intending that we'd discuss matters."

She turned her head. Their glances locked. After a while that seemed lengthy, he saw part of the tension go from her. "Thanks, Commander," she said. Did her lips flutter the ghostliest bit upward? "Coffee and a sandwich 'ud taste well, for truth."

Flandry got on the intercom to the galley. She refused a cigaret but said she didn't mind if he smoked. He inhaled several times before he said, fast:

"I'm afraid an escort destroyer leaves something to be desired in the way of accommodations. You'll have this cabin, of course. I'll move in with the mates; one of them can throw a pad on the deck. But I'll have to leave my clothes and so forth where they are. I hope the steward and I won't disturb you too badly, trotting in and out. You can take your meals here or in the wardroom, as you prefer. I'll see you get some spare coveralls or whatever to wear—sorry I didn't think to lay in a female outfit—and I'll clear a drawer to keep them in. A propos which—" he rose and opened one in his desk— "I'll leave this unlocked. It has the nonsecret items. Including a souvenir of mine." He took out a Merseian war knife. "Know how to handle this cheap and chippy chopper? I can demonstrate. It's not much use if you get in the way of a bullet, a blast, a stun beam, et cetera. But you'd be surprised

44

what it can do at close quarters." Again he caught her gaze. "Do be careful with it, my lady," he said low. "You've nothing to fear on my ship. The situation might alter. But I'd hate to think you'd gotten reckless with my souvenir and bowed out of the universe when there was no real need."

The breath hissed between her teeth. Color and pallor chased each other across her face. The hand she reached out for the knife wavered. She let it fall, raised it back to her eyes, clenched the remaining fist, and fought not to weep.

Flandry turned his back and browsed through a full-size copy of a translated *Genji Monogatori* that he'd brought along to pass the time. The snack arrived. When he had closed the door on the messman and set the tray on his desk, Kathryn McCormac was her own captain again.

"You're a strider, sir," she told him. He cocked his brows. "Aenean word," she explained. "A strong, good man . . . let me say a gentleman."

He stroked his mustache. "A gentleman manqué, perhaps." He sat back down on the bunk. Their knees brushed. "No business discussion over food. Abominable perversion, that." She flinched. "Would you care for music?" he asked hastily. "My tastes are plebeian, but I've been careful to learn what's considered high art." He operated a selector. *Eine Kleine Nachtmusik* awoke in joy.

"That's beautiful," she said when she had finished eating. "Terran?"

"Pre-spaceflight. There's a deal of antiquarianism in the inner Empire these days, revival of everything from fencing to allemands—uh, sport with swords and a class of dances. Wistfulness about eras more picturesque, less cruel and complicated. Not that they really were, I'm sure. It's only that their troubles are safely buried."

"And we've yet to bury ours." She drained her cup and clashed it down on the bare plate. "If they don't shovel us under first. Let's talk, Dominic Flandry."

"If you feel up to it." He started a fresh cigaret.

"I'd better. Time's none too long 'fore you must decide what to do 'bout me." The dark-blonde head lifted. "I feel 'freshed. Liefer attack my griefs than slump."

"Very well, my lady." *Wish I had a pretty regional accent.*

"Why'd you rescue me?" she asked gently.

He studied the tip of his cigaret. "Wasn't quite a rescue," he said.

Once more the blood left her countenance. "From Aaron Snelund," she whispered, "anything's a rescue."

"Bad?"

45

"I'd've killed myself, come the chance. Didn't get it. So I tried to keep sane by plannin' ways to kill him." She strained her fingers against each other until she noticed she was doing so. "Hugh's habit," she mumbled, pulled her hands free and made them both into fists.

"You may win a little revenge." Flandry sat straight. "Listen my lady. I'm a field agent in Intelligence. I was dispatched to investigate Sector Alpha Crucis. It occurred to me you could tell things that nobody else would. That's why you're here. Now I can't officially take your unsupported word, and I won't use methods like hypnoprobing to squeeze the facts out against your will. But if you lie to me, it's worse than if you keep silence. Worse for us both, seeing that I want to help you."

Steadiness had returned to her. She came of a hardy breed. "I'll not lie," she promised. "As to whether I'll speak at all . . . depends. Is it truth what I heard, my man's in revolt?"

"Yes. We're trailing a fleet whose mission is to defeat the rebels, seize and occupy the planets that support them—which includes your home, my lady."

"And you're with the Imperialists?"

"I'm an officer of the Terran Empire, yes."

"So's Hugh. He . . . he never wanted . . . anything but the good of the race—every race everywhere. If you'd think the matter through, I 'spect you yourself 'ud—"

"Don't count on that, my lady. But I'll listen to whatever you care to tell me."

She nodded. "I'll speak what I know. Afterward, when I'm stronger, you can give me a light 'probe and be sure I'm not swittlin'. I believe I can trust you'll use the machine just for confirmation, not for pryin' deeper."

"You can."

In spite of her sorrow, Flandry felt excitement sharpen each sense and riot in his blood. *By Pluto's single icy ball, I am on a live trail!*

She chose words and uttered them, in a flat tone but with no further hesitation. As she spoke, her face congealed into a mask.

"Hugh never planned any treason. I'd've known. He got me cleared for top security so we could also talk together 'bout his work. Sometimes I'd give him an idea. We were both murderin' mad over what Snelund's goons were doin'. Civilized worlds like Aeneas didn't suffer worse'n upratcheted taxes at first. Later, bit by bit, we saw fines, confiscations, political arrests—more and more—and when a secret police was officially installed— But that was mild compared

46

to some of the backward planets. *We* had connections, we could eventu'ly raise a zoosny on Terra, even if Snelund was a pet of the Emperor's. Those poor primitives, though—

"Hugh wrote back. To start with, he got reprimands for interferin' with civilian affairs. But gradu'ly the seriousness of his charges must've percolated through the bureaucracy. He started gettin' replies from the High Admiralty, askin' for more exact information. That was by Naval courier. We couldn't trust the mails any longer. He and I spent this year collectin' facts—depositions, photographs, audits, everything needed to make a case nobody could overlook. We were goin' to Terra in person and deliver the microfile.

"Snelund got wind. We'd taken care, but we were amateurs at sneakery, and you can't dream how poisonous horrible 'tis, havin' secret police 'round, never knowin' when you dare talk free. . . . He wrote offici'ly askin' Hugh to come discuss plans for defendin' the outermost border systems. Well, they had been havin' trouble, and Hugh's not a man who could leave without doin' something for them. I was more scared than him of a bounceplay, but I went along. We always stayed close together, those last days. I did tip the hand to Hugh's chief aide, one of my family's oldest friends, Captain Oliphant. He should stand alert in case of treachery.

"We stayed at the palace. Normal for high-rankin' visitors. Second night, as we were 'bout to turn in, a detachment of militia arrested us.

"I was taken to Snelund's personal suite. Never mind what came next. After a while, though, I noticed he could be gotten to boast. No need for pretendin' I'd changed my mind 'bout him. Contrary: he liked to see me hurtin'. But that was the way to play, then. Show hurt at the right times. I didn't really think I'd ever pass on what he told me. He said I'd leave with my mind scrubbed out of my brain. But hope— How glad I am now for grabbin' that one percent of hope!"

She stopped. Her eyes were reptile dry and did not appear to see Flandry.

"I never imagined he intended his gubernatorial antics for a full-time career," the man said, most softly. "What's his plan?"

"Return. Back to the throne. And become the puppeteer behind the Emperor."

"Hm. Does His Majesty know this?"

"Snelund claimed the two've them plotted it before he left, and've kept in touch since."

Flandry felt a sting. His cigaret had burned down to his fingers. He chucked it into the disposer and started a new

47

one. "I hardly believe our lord Josip has three brain cells to click together," he murmured. "He might have a pair, that occasionally impact soggily. But of course, brother Snelund will have made our lord feel like a monstrous clever fellow. That's part of the manipulation."

She noticed him then. "You said that?"

"If you report me, I could get broken for *lèse majesté*," Flandry admitted. "Somehow I doubt you will."

"Surely not! 'Cause you—" She checked herself.

He thought: *I didn't mean to lead her up any garden paths. But it seems I did, if she thinks maybe I'll join her man's pathetic revolt. Well, it'll make her more cooperative, which serves the Cause, and happier for a few days, if that's doing her any favor.* He said:

"I can see part of the machinery. The Emperor wants dear Aaron back. Dear Aaron points out that this requires extracting large sums from Sector Alpha Crucis. With those, he can bribe, buy elections, propagandize, arrange events, maybe purchase certain assassinations . . . till he has a Policy Board majority on his side.

"*Ergo*, word gets passed from the throne to various powerful, handpicked men. The facts about Snelund's governorship are to be suppressed as much as possible, the investigation of them delayed as long as possible and hampered by every available trick when finally it does roll. Yes. I'd begun to suspect it on my own hook."

He frowned. "But a scandal of these dimensions can't be concealed forever," he said. "Enough people will resign themselves to having Snelund for a gray eminence that his scheme will work—*unless* they understand what he's done out here. Then they might well take measures, if only because they fear what he could do to them.

"Snelund isn't stupid, worse luck. Maybe no big, spectacular warriors or statesmen can topple him. But a swarm of drab little accountants and welfare investigators isn't that easily fended off. He must have a plan for dealing with them too. What is it?"

"Civil war," she answered.

"Huh?" Flandry dropped his cigaret.

"Goad till he's got a rebellion," she said bleakly. "Suppress it in such a way that no firm evidence of anything remains.

"He'd soonest not have this fleet win a clear victory. A prolonged campaign, with planets comin' under attack, would give him his chaos free. But s'posin', which I doubt, your admiral can beat Hugh at a stroke, there'll still be 'pacification'

48

left for his mercenaries, and they'll have their instructions how to go 'bout it.

"Afterward he'll disband them, 'long with his overlord corps. He recruited from the scum of everywhere else in the Empire, and they'll scatter back through it and vanish automatic'ly. He'll blame the revolt on subversion, and claim to be the heroic leader who saved this frontier."

She sighed. "Oh, yes," she finished, "he knows there'll be loose ends. But he doesn't 'spect they'll be important: 'speci'ly as he reckons to supply a lot of them himself."

"A considerable risk," Flandry mused. "But Krishna, what stakes!"

"The Merseian crisis was a grand chance," Kathryn McCormac said. "Attention bent yonder and most of the local fleet gone. He wanted Hugh out of the way 'cause Hugh was dangerous to him, but also 'cause he hoped this'd clear the path for tormentin' Aeneas till Aeneas rose and touched off the fission. Hugh was more'n chief admiral for the sector. He's Firstman of Ilion, which puts him as high on the planet as anybody 'cept the resident. Our Cabinet could only name him an 'expert advisor' under the law, but toward the end he was Speaker in everything save title and led its resistance to Snelund's tools. And Aeneas has tradition'ly set the tone for all human colonies out here, and a good many nonhumans besides."

Life flowed back. Her nostrils flared. "Snelund never looked, though, for havin' Hugh to fight!"

Flandry ground the dropped butt under his heel. Presently he told her, "I'm afraid the Imperium cannot allow a rebellion to succeed, regardless of how well-intentioned."

"But they'll know the truth," she protested.

"At best, they'll get your testimony," he said. "You had a bad time. Frequent drugging and brain-muddling, among other things, right?" He saw her teeth catch her lip. "I'm sorry to remind you, my lady, but I'd be sorrier to leave you in a dream that's due to vaporize. The mere fact that you believe you heard Snelund tell you these schemes does not prove one entropic thing. Confusion—paranoia—deliberate planting of false memories by agents who meant to discredit the governor—any smart advocate, any suborned psychiatrist, could rip your story to ions. You wouldn't carry it past the first investigator screening witnesses for a court of inquiry."

She stared at him as if he had struck her. "Don't you believe me?"

"I want to," Flandry said. "Among other reasons, because your account indicates where and how to look for evidence that can't be tiddlywinked away. Yes, I'll be shooting message capsules with coded dispatches off to various strategic destinations."

"Not goin' home yourself?"

"Why should I, when my written word has better odds of being taken seriously than your spoken one? Not that the odds are much to wager on." Flandry marshalled his thoughts. They were reluctant to stand and be identified. "You see," he said slowly, "bare assertions are cheap. Solid proofs are needed. A mountain of them, if you're to get anywhere against an Imperial favorite and the big men who stand to grow bigger by supporting him. And . . . Snelund is quite right . . . a planet that's been fought over with modern weapons isn't apt to have a worthwhile amount of evidence left on it. No, I think this ship's best next move is to Aeneas."

"What?"

"We'll try a parley with your husband, my lady. I hope you can talk him into quitting. Then afterward they may turn up what's required for the legal frying of Aaron Snelund."

VI

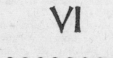

The star Virgil is type F7, slightly more massive than Sol, half again as luminous, with a higher proportion of ultraviolet in its emission. Aeneas is the fourth of its planets, completing an orbit in 1.73 standard years at an average distance of 1.50 astronomical units and thus receiving two-thirds the irradiation that Terra gets. Its mean diameter is 10,700 kilometers, its mass 0.45 Terra, hence gravity on the surface equals 0.635 g. This suffices to retain a humanly breathable atmosphere, comparable on the lowest levels to Denver Complex and on the highest to the Peruvian altiplano. (You must bear in mind that a weak pull means a correspondingly small density gradient, plus orogenic forces insufficient to raise very tall mountains.) Through ages, water molecules have ascended in the thin air and been cracked by energetic quanta; the hydrogen has escaped to space, the oxygen that has not has tended to unite with minerals. Thus little remains of the former oceans, and deserts have become extensive.

The chief original inducement to colonize was scientific: the unique races on the neighbor planet Dido, which itself was no world whereon a man would want to keep his family. Of course, various other kinds of people settled too; but the explorer-intellectuals dominated. Then the Troubles came, and the Aeneans had to survive as best they could, cut off, for generations. They adapted.

The result was a stock more virile and gifted, a society more patriotic and respectful of learning, than most. After civilization returned to the Alpha Crucis region, Aeneas inevitably became its local leader. To the present day, the University of Virgil in Nova Roma drew students and scholars from greater distances than you might expect.

Eventually the Imperium decided that proper organization of this critical sector demanded an end to Aenean independence. Intrigue and judicious force accomplished it. A hundred years later, some resentment lingered, though the ordinary dweller agreed that incorporation had been desirable on the whole and the planet supplied many outstanding men to the Terran armed services.

Its military-intellectual tradition continued. Every Aenean trained in arms—including women, who took advantage of reduced weight. The old baronial families still led. Their titles might not be recognized by the Imperial peerage, but were by their own folk; they kept their strongholds and broad lands; they furnished more than their share of officers and professors. In part this was due to their tendency to choose able spouses, regardless of rank. On its upper levels, Aenean society was rather formal and austere, though it had its sports and holidays and other depressurizing institutions. On its lower levels there was more jollity, but also better manners than you could find on Terra.

Thus a description, cataloguing several facts and omitting the really significant one: that to four hundred million human beings, Aeneas was home.

The sun was almost down. Rays ran gold across the Antonine Seabed, making its groves and plantations a patchwork of bluish-green and shadows, burning on its canals, molten in

51

the mists that curled off a salt marsh. Eastward, the light smote crags and cliffs where the ancient continental shelf of Ilion lifted a many-tiered, wind-worn intricacy of purple, rose, ocher, tawny, black up to a royal blue sky. The outer moon, Lavinia, was a cold small horn on top of that mass.

The wind was cold too. Its whittering blent with the soft roar of a waterfall, the clop of hoofs and creak and jingle of harness as horses wound along a steep upward trail. Those were Aenean horses, shaggy, rangy, their low-gravity gait looking less rapid than it was. Hugh McCormac rode one. His three sons by his first wife accompanied him. Ostensibly they had been hunting spider wolves, but they hadn't found any and didn't care. The unspoken real reason had been to fare forth together across this land that was theirs. They might not have another chance.

A vulch wheeled into view, wings across heaven. John McCormac lifted his rifle. His father glanced behind. "No, don't," he said. "Let it live."

"Save death for the Terries, hey?" asked Bob. At nine years of age—16 standard—he was a bit loud about his discovery that the universe wasn't quite as simple as they pretended in school.

He'll outgrow that, McCormac thought. *He's a good boy. They all are, like their sisters. How could they help being, with Ramona for mother?* "I don't hold with killing anything unnecessarily," he said. "That isn't what war is about."

"Well, I don't know," Colin put in. He was the oldest. Since he would therefore be the next Firstman, family custom had kept him from joining the service. (Hugh McCormac had only succeeded when his elder brother was caught in a sand hell and died childless.) Perhaps his planetographic researches in the Virgilian System had not satisfied every inborn impulse. "You weren't here, Father, when the revolution reached Nova Roma. But I saw crowds—plain, kindly citizens—hound Snelund's political police down the streets, catch them, string them up, and beat them to death. And it felt right. It still does, when you think what they'd done earlier."

"Snelund himself'll be a while dyin', if I catch him," John said hotly.

"No!" McCormac snapped. "You'll not sink yourself to his ways. He'll be killed as cleanly as we kill any other mad dog. His associates will have fair trials. There *are* degrees of guilt."

"If we can find the lice," Bob said.

McCormac thought of the wilderness of suns and worlds

52

where his life had passed, and said, "Probably most will succeed in disappearing. What of it? We'll have more urgent work than revenge."

They rode silent for a while. The trail debouched on one of the steplike plateaus and joined a paved road to Windhome. Soil lay deep, washed down from the heights, and vegetation flourished, in contrast to a few dwarf bushes on the eroded slopes. Trava decked the ground almost as luxuriantly as it did the seabed. Mainly it was fire trava here, the serrated leaves edged with scarlet; but the sword kind bristled and the plume kind nodded. Each type was curling up for the night as temperature dropped, to form a springy heat-conserving mat. Trees grew about, not only the low iron-hard native sorts but imported oak, cedar, and rasmin. The wind carried their fragrances. Some ways to the right, smoke blew from a farmer's stone cottage. Robotized latifundia weren't practical on Aeneas, and McCormac was glad of that; he felt in his bones that a healthy society needed yeomen.

Colin clucked to his horse and drew alongside. His sharp young face looked unhappy. "Father—" He stopped.

"Go ahead," McCormac invited.

"Father . . . do you think . . . do you really think we can pull it off?"

"I don't know," McCormac said. "We'll try like men, that's all."

"But—makin' you Emperor—"

McCormac felt anew how pitifully little chance he'd had to speak with his nearest, since his rescuers brought him home: too much to do, and each scant hour when something wasn't clamoring for attention, the body toppled into sleep. He had actually stolen this one day.

"Please don't imagine I want the job," he said. "You haven't been on Terra. I have. I don't like it. I was never happier than when they reassigned me back where I belong."

Imperial routine, passed over his mind. Rotate careerists through a series of regions; but in the end, whenever feasible, return them to the sectors they came from. Theory: they'll defend their birthhomes more fiercely than some clutch of planets foreign to them. Practice: when revolt erupted, many Navy personnel, like civilians, discovered that those homes meant more to them than a Terra most of them had never seen. Problem: if I win, should I discontinue the practice, as Josip doubtless will if his admirals win?

"But why, then?" Colin asked.

"What else could I do?" McCormac replied.

"Well . . . freedom—"

53

"No. The Empire is not so far decayed that it'll allow itself to be broken apart. And even if it were, I wouldn't. Don't you see, it's the single thing that stands between civilization —our civilization—and the Long Night?

"As for armed protest, it might stimulate policy changes, but the Imperium could not pardon the ringleaders. That'd invite everybody with a grudge to start shooting, and spell the end as clearly as partition would. And besides—" McCormac's knuckles stood white where he grasped the reins— "it wouldn't get Kathryn back, if any hope remains of that."

"So you aim to preserve the Empire, but take it over," Colin said quickly. His desire to guide his father's thoughts off his stepmother's captivity was so obvious that McCormac's heart writhed. "I'm with you. You know that. I honestly think you'd give it new life—the best Emperor we've had since Isamu the Great, maybe since Manuel I himself— and I'm layin' not just me, but my wife and son on the board for you—but can it be done?" He waved at the sky. "The Empire's that huge!"

As if at a signal, Virgil went down. The Aenean atmosphere held no twilight worth mentioning. Alpha and Beta Crucis blazed forth, then almost instantly thousands more and the frosty bridge of the Milky Way. The land mass on the right became utterly black, but Lavinia silvered the sea bottom under the left-hand cliffs. A tadmouse piped into the mordant wind.

McCormac said: "The revolution has to have a leader, and I'm its choice. Let's have no false modesty. I control the Cabinet on the principal world of this sector. I can prove by the record I'm the top Naval strategist the Empire has. My men know I'm strict about things that matter, compassionate about the rest, and always try to be fair. So do a hundred planets, human and nonhuman. It'd be no service to anyone if I claimed different."

"But how—" Colin's voice trailed off. Moonlight glimmered along his leather jacket and off his silver-mounted saddle.

"We'll take control of this sector," McCormac told him. "That's largely a matter of defeating the Josipist forces. Once we've done it, every significant community in a ten-parsec radius will come over to us. Afterward . . . I don't like the idea myself, but I know where and how to get barbarian allies. Not the few Darthan ships I've already engaged; no, really wild warriors from well outside the border. Don't worry, I won't let them plunder and I won't let them settle,

54

even if they'll swear allegiance. They'll be hirelings paid from tax monies.

"The whole Imperial fleet can't ever come against us. It has too many other duties. If we work fast and hard, we'll be in shape to throw back whatever does attack.

"Beyond that—I can't predict. I'm hoping we'll have a well-governed region to show. I'm hoping that will underline our message: an end to corruption and tyranny, a fresh start under a fresh dynasty, long-overdue reforms. . . . What we need is momentum, the momentum of a snowball. Then all the guns in the Empire can't stop us: because most of them will be on our side."

Why a snowball? jeered his mind. *Who knows snow on Aeneas, except a thin drift in polar winter?*

They rounded a cluster of trees and spied the castle. Windhome stood on what had once been a cape and now thrust out into air, with a dizzying drop beneath. Lights glowed yellow from its bulk, outlining dark old walls and battlements. The Wildfoss River brawled past in cataracts.

But McCormac did not see this immediately. His eyes had gone to the flat Antonine horizon, far below and far away. Above a last greenish trace of sunset, beneath a wan flicker of aurora, burned pure white Dido, the evening star.

Where Kathryn worked, xenologist in its jungles, till that time I met her, five years ago (no, three Aenean years; have I really been so long in the Empire that I've forgotten the years of our planet?) and we loved and were married.

And you always wished for children of your own, Kathryn, dyuba, and we were going to have them, but there were always public troubles that ought to be settled first; and tonight — He thanked his iron God that the sun of Llynathawr was not visible in these latitudes. His throat was thick with the need to weep. Instead, he spurred his horse to a gallop.

The road crossed cultivated fields before it reached Windhome's portal. A caravan of tinerants had established itself on the meadow in front. Their trucks were parked aside, lost in gloom; light from the castle fell only on gaily striped tents, fluttering flags, half-erected booths. Men, women, children, packed around campfires, stopped their plangent music and stamping dances to give the lord of the manor a hail as he rode by. Tomorrow these tatterdemalion wanderers would open their carnival . . . and it would draw merrymakers from a hundred kilometers around . . . though the fist of the Imperium was already slamming forward.

I don't understand, McCormac thought.

Horseshoes rang in the courtyard. A groom caught his reins. He jumped to the ground. Guards were about, the new-come Navy personnel and the liveried family retainers strutting with jealous glances at each other. Edgar Oliphant hurried from the keep. Though McCormac, as Emperor, had raised him to admiral, he hadn't yet bothered to change the captain's star on either shoulder. He had merely added a brassard in the Ilian colors to the tunic that snugged around his stocky form.

"Welcome back, sir!" he exclaimed. "I was 'bout to dispatch a search party."

McCormac achieved a laugh. "Good cosmos, do you think my boys and I can get lost on our ancestral lands?"

"N-no. No, sir. But 'tis, well, if you'll 'scuse me, sir, 'tis foolish for you to run loose with not a single security escort."

McCormac shrugged. "I'll have to endure that later, on Terra. Leave me my privacy a while." Peering closer: "You've something to tell me."

"Yes, sir. Word came in two hours ago. If the admiral, uh, the Emperor will come with me?"

McCormac tried to give his sons a rueful look. He was secretly not sorry to have his awareness taken from the orbit into which it had fallen—again.

The ancient dignity of the Firstman's office had vanished of recent weeks in a clutter of new gear: communication, computation, electronic files and scanners. McCormac sank into a chair behind his battered desk; that at least was familiar. "Well?" he said.

Oliphant closed the door. "The initial report's been confirmed by two more scouts," he said. "The Imperial armada is movin'. 'Twill be here inside three days." It made no difference whether he meant the standard period or the 20-hour rotation of Aeneas.

McCormac nodded. "I didn't doubt the first crew," he said. "Our plans still stand. Tomorrow, 0600 Nova Roma time, I board my flagship. Two hours later, our forces depart."

"But are you certain, sir, the enemy won't occupy Aeneas?"

"No. I would be surprised, though, if he did. What gain? My kinfolk and I won't be around to seize. I've arranged for the enemy to learn that when he arrives. What else can he make a prize of on Aeneas, till the fighting's past? Whoever wins in space can mop up the planets soon enough. Until then, why commit strength badly needed elsewhere, to grip a spearwasp's nest like this world? If he does occupy, then he

56

does. But I expect he'll leave the Virgilian System the instant he discovers we aren't trying to defend it, we're off to grab the real trophy—Satan."

"Your screenin' forces, however—" Oliphant said dubiously.

"Do you mean protection for offplanet bases like Port Frederiksen? A light vessel each, mostly to guard against possible casual destructiveness."

"No, sir. I'm thinkin' of your interplanetary patrols. What effect 'ull they have?"

"They're just Darthan mercenaries. They have no other purpose than to mislead the enemy, gaining time for our fleet," McCormac said. *Have I really not made it clear to him before now? What else have I overlooked since the avalanche hit me?— No, it's all right, he's simply been too engaged with administrative details on the ground.* "A few vessels posted in local space, with orders to attack any Josipist craft they may spot. Those'll be scouts, of course, weakly armed, easily defeated. The survivors among them will carry the news back. I know Pickens' style of thinking. He'll be convinced we intend to make a fight of it at Virgil, and proceed ultra-cautiously, and therefore not detect us on our way off to Beta Crucis." *Oh, good old Dave Pickens, who always brought flowers for Kathryn when we invited you to dinner, must I indeed use against you the things I learned when we were friends?*

"Well, you're the Emperor, sir." Oliphant gestured at the machines hemming them in. "Plenty of business today. We handled it how we could in Staff, but some items seem to require your attention."

"I'll give them a look-over right away, before eating," McCormac said. "Stay available afterward, in case I need to consult."

"Aye, sir." Oliphant saluted and left.

McCormac didn't retrieve the communications at once. Instead, he went out on a balcony. It opened on the cliff and the rich eastern bottomlands. Creusa, the inner moon, was about due to rise. He filled his lungs with dry chill and waited.

Nearly full, the satellite exploded over the horizon. The shadows it cast moved noticeably; and as it hurtled, he could watch the phase change. Drowned in that living white light, the Antonine appeared to get back its vanished waters. It was as if phantom waves ran across those reaches and surf beat once more on the foot of Windhome ness.

57

You used to say that, Kathryn. You loved these moments best, in the whole year of our world. Dyuba, dyuba, will you ever see them again?

VII

When Virgil showed a perceptible disc without magnification, *Asieneuve* went out of hyperdrive and accelerated inward on gravs. Every sensor strained at maximum receptivity; and nothing came through save an endless seething of cosmic energies.

"Not so much as a radio broadcast?" Flandry asked.

"Not yet, sir," Rovian's voice replied.

Flandry turned off the intercom. "I should be on the bridge myself," he muttered. "What am I doing in my—your cabin?"

"Gatherin' intelligence," the woman said with a faint smile.

"If only I were! Why total silence? Has the whole system been evacuated?"

"Hardly. But they must know the enemy'll arrive in a couple days. Hugh's a genius at deployin' scouts. He is at most things."

Flandry's gaze sharpened on her. Too restless to sit, too cramped to pace, he stood by the door and drummed fingers on it. Kathryn McCormac occupied the chair. She appeared almost calm.

But then, she had done little except sleep, between his first talk with her and this one. It had gone far toward healing her in body and, he hoped, at least a small distance toward knitting the wounds that had been torn in her mind. The time had, however, given him a bad case of the crawlies. It had been no easy decision to race ahead of the fleet, the whole

58

way at top quasispeed, bearing his prisoner to the rebel chieftain. He had no hint of authority to negotiate. His action could only be defended on the freest imaginable interpretation of his orders; wouldn't it be valuable to sound out the great insurrectionist, and didn't the wife's presence offer a windfall opportunity to do so?

Why does it bother me to hear love in her voice? Flandry wondered.

He said, "My own genius is in glibness. But that won't get my stern out of the sling if this maneuver doesn't show some kind of profit."

The chrysocolla eyes beneath the amber bangs focused on him. "You'll not make Hugh yield," she warned. "I'd never ask him to, no matter what. They'd shoot him, wouldn't they?"

Flandry shifted his stance. Sweat prickled under his arms. "Well—a plea for leniency—"

He had seldom heard as grim a laugh. "Of your courtesy, Commander, spare us both. I may be a colonial, and I may've spent my adult life 'fore marriage doin' scientific studies on a breed of bein's that're scarcely more concerned with mankind than Ymirites are . . . but I did study history and politics, and bein' the Fleet Admiral's lady did give me a lot to observe. 'Tis not possible for the Imperium to grant Hugh a pardon." Briefly, her tone faltered. "And I . . . 'ud rather see him dead . . . than a brain-channeled slave or a lifelong prisoner . . . a crag bull like him."

Flandry took out a cigaret, though his palate was scorched leather. "The idea, my lady," he said, "is that you'll tell him what you've learned. If nothing else, he may then avoid playing Snelund's game. He can refuse to give battle on or around those planets that Snelund would like to see bombarded."

"But without bases, sources of supply—" She drew a shaken breath. It bulged out the coverall she wore in a way to trouble Flandry. "Well, we can talk, of course," she said in misery. The regained strength fell from her. She half reached toward him. "Commander . . . if you could let me go—"

Flandry looked away and shook his head. "I'm sorry, my lady. You've a capital charge against you, and you've been neither acquitted nor pardoned. The single excuse I could give for releasing you would be that it bought your husband's surrender, and you tell me that's unthinkable." He dragged smoke into his lungs and remembered vaguely that he ought soon to get an anticancer booster. "Understand, you won't be turned back to Snelund. I'd join the rebellion too before per-

59

mitting that. You'll come with me to Terra. What you can relate of your treatment at Snelund's hands, and his brags to you . . . well, it may cause him difficulty. At a minimum, it ought to gain you the sympathy of men who're powerful enough to protect you."

Glancing her way again, he was shocked to see how the blood had left her face. Her eyes stared blank, and beads of perspiration glittered forth. "My lady!" He flung the cigaret aside, made two steps, and stooped above her. "What's wrong?" he laid a palm on her brow. It was cold. So were her hands, when his slipped as if of themselves down her shoulders and arms. He hunkered in front and chafed them. "My lady—"

Kathryn McCormac stirred. "A stimpill?" she whispered.

Flandry debated calling the ship's medic, decided not to, and gave her the tablet and a tumbler of water. She gulped. When he saw the corpse color going and the breath becoming steady, it rejoiced in him.

"I'm sorry," she said, scarcely audible above the murmur of the ship. "The memory bounced out at me too quick."

"I said the wrong thing," he stammered, contrite.

"Not your fault." She stared at the deck. He couldn't help noticing how long the lashes were against her bronze skin. "Terran mores are different from ours. To you, what happened to me was . . . unfortunate, nasty, yes, but not a befoulin' I'll never quite cleanse me of, not a thing makes me wonder if I really should want to see Hugh ever again. . . . Maybe, though, you'll understand some if I tell you how often he used drugs and brain-scramblers. Time and again, I was trapped in a nightmare where I couldn't think, wasn't me, had no will, wasn't anything but an animal doin' what he told me, to 'scape pain—"

I oughtn't to hear this, Flandry thought. *She wouldn't speak of it if her self-command had entirely returned. How can I leave?*

"My lady," he attempted, "you said a fact, that it wasn't you. You shouldn't let it count. If your husband's half the man you claim, he won't."

She sat motionless a while. The stimulol acted faster than normal on her; evidently she wasn't in the habit of using chemical crutches. At length she raised her head. The countenance was deeply flushed, but the big body seemed in repose. And she smiled.

"You *are* a strider," she said.

"Uh . . . feeling well now?"

"Better, anyways. Could we talk straight business?"

60

Flandry gusted a secret sigh of relief. A touch weak in his own knees, he sat down on the bunk and began another cigaret. "Yes, I rather urgently want to," he said. "For the proverbial nonce, we have common interests, and your information might be what lets us carry on instead of scuttling off for home and mother."

"What d'you need to know? I may not be able to answer some questions, and may refuse to answer others."

"Agreed. But let's try on a few. We've caught no trace of astronautical activity in this system. A fleet the size of Hugh McCormac's should register one way or another. If nothing else, by neutrino emission from powerplants. What's he done? He might be fairly close to the sun, keeping behind it with respect to us; or might be lying doggo a goodly distance out, like half a light-year; or might have hauled mass for some different territory altogether; or— Have you any ideas?"

"No."

"Certain you don't?"

She bridled. "If I did, would I tell?"

"Sizzle it, one destroyer doesn't make a task force! Put it this way: How can we contact him before battle commences?"

She yielded. "I don't know, and that's honest," she said, meeting his stare without wavering. "I can tell you this, whatever Hugh's plannin' 'ull be something bold and unexpected."

"Marvelous," Flandry groaned. "Well, how about the radio silence?"

"Oh, that's easier to 'splain, I think. We don't have many stations broadcastin' with enough power, at the right wavelengths, to be detectable far out. Virgil's too apt to hash them up with solar storms. Mainly we send tight beams via relay satellites. Radiophones're common—isolated villages and steadin's need them—but they natur'ly use frequencies that the ionosphere 'ull contain. Virgil gives Aeneas a mighty deep ionosphere. In short, 'tisn't hard to get 'long without the big stations, and I s'pose they're doin' it so enemy navigators 'ull have extra trouble obtainin' in-system positions."

You understand that principle too—never giving the opposition a free ride, never missing a chance to complicate his life? Flandry thought with respect. *I've known a lot of civilians, including officers' spouses, who didn't.*

"What about interplanetary communications?" he asked. "I assume you do mining and research on the sister worlds. You mentioned having been involved yourself. Think those bases were evacuated?"

"N-no. Not the main one on Dido, at least. It's self-supportin', kind of, and there's too big an investment in apparatus, records, relationships with natives." Pride rang: "I know my old colleagues. They won't abandon simply 'cause of an invasion."

"But your people may have suspended interplanetary talk during the emergency?"

"Yes, belike. 'Speci'ly since the Josipists prob'ly won't carry data on where everything is in our system. And what they can't find, they can't wreck."

"They wouldn't," Flandry protested. "Not in mere spite."

She retorted with an acrid: "How do you know what His Ex'lency may've told their admiral?"

The intercom's buzz saved him, from devising a reply. He flipped the switch. "Bridge to captain," came Rovian's thick, hissing tones. "A ship has been identified at extreme range. It appears to have started on a high-thrust intercept course to ours."

"I'll be right there." Flandry stood. "You heard, my lady?"

She nodded. He thought he could see how she strained to hold exterior calm.

"Report to Emergency Station Three," he said. "Have the yeoman on duty fit you with a spacesuit and outline combat procedure. When we close with that chap, everyone goes into armor and harness. Three will be your post. It's near the middle of the hull, safest place, not that that's a very glowing encomium. Tell the yeoman that I'll want your helmet transceiver on a direct audiovisual link to the bridge and the comshack. Meanwhile, stay in this cabin, out of the way."

"Do you 'spect danger?" she asked quietly.

"I'd better not expect anything else." He departed.

The bridge viewscreens showed Virgil astonishingly grown. *Asieneuve* had entered the system with a high relative true velocity, and her subsequent acceleration would have squashed her crew were it not for the counteraction of the interior gee-field. Its radiance stopped down in simulacrum, the sun burned amidst a glory of corona and zodiacal light.

Flandry assumed the command chair. Rovian said: "I suppose the vessel was orbiting, generators at minimum, until it detected us. If we wish to rendezvous with it near Aeneas"— a claw pointed at a ruddy spark off the starboard quarter— "we must commence deceleration."

"M-m-m, I think not." Flandry rubbed his chin. "If I were that skipper, I'd be unhappy about a hostile warship close to my home planet, whether or not she's a little one and says she wants to parley. For all he knows, our messages are off tapes and there's nobody here but us machines, boss." He didn't need to spell out what devastation could be wrought, first by any nuclear missiles that didn't get intercepted, finally by a suicide plunge of the ship's multiple tons at perhaps a hundred kilometers a second. "When they've got only one important city, a kamikaze is worth fretting about. He could get a wee bit impulsive."

"What does the captain mean to do, then?"

Flandry activated an astronomical display. The planet-dots, orbit-circles, and vector-arrows merely gave him a rough idea of conditions, but refinements were the navigation department's job. "Let's see. The next planet inward, Dido they call it, past quadrature but far enough from conjunction that there'd be no ambiguity about our aiming for it. And a scientific base . . . cool heads . . . yes, I think it'd be an earnest of pious intentions if we took station around Dido. Set course for the third planet, Citizen Rovian."

"Aye, sir." The directives barked forth, the calculations were made, the engine sang on a deeper note as its power began to throttle down speed.

Flandry prepared a tape announcing his purposes. "If discussion is desired prior to our reaching terminus, please inform. We will keep a receiver tuned on the standard band," he finished, and ordered continuous broadcast.

Time crept by. "What if we are not allowed to leave this system afterward?" Rovian said once in Eriau.

"Chance we take," Flandry replied. "Not too big a risk, I judge, considering the hostage we hold. Besides, in spite of our not releasing her to him, I trust friend McCormac will be duly appreciative of our having gotten her away from that swine Snelund. . . . No, I shouldn't insult the race of swine, should I? His parents were brothers."

"What do you really expect to accomplish?"

"God knows, and He hasn't seen fit to declassify the information. Maybe nothing. Maybe opening some small channel, some way of moderating the war if not halting it. Keep the bridge for ten minutes, will you? If I can't sneak off and get a smoke, I'll implode."

"Can you not indulge here?"

"The captain on a human ship isn't supposed to have human failings, they hammered into me when I was a caydet. I'll have too many explanations to invent for my superiors as is."

Rovian emitted a noise that possibly corresponded to a chuckle.

The hours trickled past. Virgil swelled in the screens. Rovian reported: "Latest data on the other ship indicate it has decided we are bound for Dido, and plans to get there approximately simultaneously. No communication with it thus far, though it must now be picking up our broadcast."

"Odd. Anything on the vessel herself?" Flandry asked.

"Judging from its radiations and our radar, it has about the same tonnage and power as us but is not any Naval model."

"No doubt the Aeneans have pressed everything into service that'll fly, from broomsticks to washtubs. Well, that's a relief. They can't contemplate fighting a regular unit like ours."

"Unless the companion—" Rovian referred to a second craft, detected a while ago after she swung past the sun.

"You told me that one can't make Dido till hours after we do, except by going hyper; and I doubt her captain is so hot for Dido that he'll do that, this deep in a gravitational well. No, she must be another picket, brought in on a just-in-case basis."

Nevertheless, he called for armor and battle stations when *Asieneuve* neared the third planet.

It loomed gibbous before him, a vast, roiling ball of snowy cloud. No moon accompanied it. The regional *Pilot's Manual and Ephemeris* described a moderately eccentric orbit whose radius vector averaged about one astronomical unit; a mass, diameter, and hence surface gravity very slightly less than Terra's; a rotation once in eight hours and 47 minutes around an axis tilted at a crazy 38 degrees; an oxynitrogen atmosphere hotter and denser than was good for men, but breathable by them; a d-amino biochemistry, neither poisonous nor nourishing to humankind—That was virtually the whole entry. The worlds were too numerous; not even the molecules of the reel could encode much information on any but the most important.

When he had donned his own space gear, aside from gauntlets and closing the faceplate, Flandry put Kathryn McCormac on circuit. Her visage in the screen, looking out of the helmet, made him think of warrior maidens in archaic books he had read. "Well?" she asked.

"I'd like to get in touch with your research base," he said, "but how the deuce can I find it under that pea soup?"

"They may not answer your call."

"On the other hand, they may; the more likely if I beamcast so they can tell I've got them spotted. That ship closing with us is maintaining her surly silence, and— Well, if they're old chums of yours on the ground, they ought to respond to *you*."

64

She considered. "All right, I trust you, Dominic Flandry. The base, Port Frederiksen"—a brief white smile—"one of my ancestors founded it—'s on the western end of Barca, as we've named the biggest continent. Latitude 34° 5'18" north. I 'spect you can take it from there with radar."

"And thermal and magnetic and suchlike gizmos. Thanks. Stand by to talk in, oh, maybe half an hour or an hour."

Her look was grave. "I'll speak them truth."

"That'll do till we can think of something better and cheaper." Flandry switched off, but it was as if her countenance still occupied the screen. He turned to Rovian. "We'll assume an approximate hundred-minute orbit till we've identified the base, then move out to a synchronous orbit above it."

The exec switched his space-armored tail. "Sir, that means the rebel ship will find us barely outside atmosphere."

"And it's useful to be higher in a planet's field. Well, didn't you last inform me she's coming in too fast to manage less than a hyperbolic orbit?"

"Yes, sir, unless it can brake much quicker than we can."

"Her master's suspicious. He must intend to whip by in a hurry, lest we throw things at him. That's not unnatural. I'd be nervous of any enemy destroyer myself, if I were in a converted freighter or whatever she is. When he sees we're amiable, he'll take station—by which time, with luck, we'll be another ten or fifteen thousand kilometers out and talking to the scientific lads."

"Aye, sir. Have I the captain's permission to order screen fields extended at full strength?"

"Not till we've located Port Frederiksen. They'd bedbug the instruments. But otherwise, except for the detector team, absolute combat readiness, of course."

Am I right? If I'm wrong— The loneliness of command engulfed Flandry. He tried to fend it off by concentrating on approach maneuvers.

Eventually *Asieneuve* was falling free around Dido. The cessation of noise and quiver was like sudden deafness. The planet filled the starboard screens, dazzling on the dayside, dark when the ship swung around into night, save where aurora glimmered and lightning wove webs. That stormy atmosphere hindered investigation. Flandry found himself gripping his chair arms till he drove the blood from his fingernails.

"We could observe the other ship optically now, sir," Rovian said, "were this disc not in between."

"It would be," Flandry said. The exec's uneasiness had begun to gnaw in him.

An intercom voice said: "I think we've found it, sir. Latitude's right, infrared pattern fits a continent to east and an ocean to west, radar suggests buildings, we may actually have gotten a neutrino blip from a nuclear installation. Large uncertainty factor in everything, though, what with the damned interference. Shall we repeat, next orbit?"

"No," Flandry said, and realized he spoke needlessly loud. He forced levelness into his tone. "Lock on radar. Pilot, keep inside that horizon while we ascend. We'll go synchronous and take any further readings from there." *I want to be under thrust when that actor arrives in his deaf-mute role. And, oh, yes,* "Maximum screen fields, Citizen Rovian."

The officer's relief was obvious as he issued commands. The ship stirred back to life. A shifting complex of gravitic forces lifted her in a curve that was nearer a straight line than a spiral. The planet's stormy crescent shrank a little.

"Give me a projection of the rendezvousing craft, soon as you have a line of sight," Flandry said. *I'll feel a lot cheerier after I've eyeballed her.* He made himself lean back and wait.

The vision leaped into the screen. A man yelled. Rovian hissed.

That lean shape rushing down the last kilometers had never been for peaceful use. She was simply, deceptively not of Imperial manufacture. The armament was as complete as *Asieneuve's,* and as smoothly integrated with the hull. Needle nose and rakish fins declared she was meant to traverse atmosphere more often than a corresponding Terran warship . . . as for example on her way to loot a town—

Barbarians, flashed in Flandry. *From some wild country on some wild planet, where maybe a hundred years ago they were still warring with edged iron, only somebody found advantage—military, commercial—in teaching them about spaceflight, providing them with machines and a skeleton education. . . . No wonder they haven't responded to us. Probably not one aboard knows Anglic!*

"White flare," he snapped. " 'Pax' broadcast." They must recognize the signals of peace. Hugh McCormac couldn't have engaged them, as he doubtless had, unless they'd been in some contact with his civilization.

The order was obeyed at once.

Energy stabbed blue-white out of the mercenary. Missiles followed.

Flandry heard a roar of abused metal. He struck the combat button. *Asieneuve's* response was instant. And it was the ship's own. At quarters this close, living flesh could not perceive what went on, let alone react fact enough. Her blaster cannon discharged. Her countermissiles soared to meet what had been sent against her. A second later, tubes opened to release her big birds.

Nuclear detonations raged. Electromagnetic screens could ward off the sleet of ions, but not the heat radiation and X-rays, nor the thrust of energy lances and the assault of material torpedoes. Negagrav forces could slow the latter, but not stop them. Interceptors must do that, if they could.

The barbarian had the immense advantage of high speed and high altitude relative to the planet. She was the harder target to come near, her defenses the harder to penetrate if you did.

Nonetheless, Rovian's work of years bore fruit. Abrupt flame seethed around the enemy. White-hot shrapnel fled from a place where armor plate had been. Twisted, crumpled, blackened, half melted, the rest of the ship whirled off on a cometary path around the world and back toward outer space.

But it was not possible that the Terran escape free. Tactical experts reckoned the life of a destroyer in this kind of fight as less than three minutes. Firebeams had seared and gouged through *Asieneuve's* vitals. No warhead had made the direct hit that would have killed her absolutely; but three explosions were so close that the blast from their shaped charges tore into the hull, bellowing, burning, shattering machines like porcelain, throwing men about and ripping them like red rag dolls.

Flandry saw the bridge crack open. A shard of steel went through Rovian as a circular saw cuts a tree in twain. Blood sheeted, broke into a fog of droplets in the sudden weightlessness, volatilized in the dwindling pressure, and was gone except for spattered stains. Stunned, deafened, his own blood filling nose and mouth, Flandry managed to slam shut the faceplate and draw on the gloves he had forgotten about, before the last air shrieked through the hole.

Then there was a silence. Engines dead, the destroyer reached the maximum altitude permitted by the velocity she had had, and fell back toward the planet.

VIII

~~~~~~~~~~~~

No boat remained spaceworthy. Where destruction was not total, crucial systems had been knocked out. Time was lacking to make repairs or cannibalize. One of the four craft offered a weak hope. Though its fusion generator was inoperative, its accumulators could energize the two drive cones that seemed usable; and the instruments and controls were undamaged. An aerodynamic landing might be possible. Every rated pilot was killed or wounded—but Flandry had flown combat aircraft before he transferred to the Intelligence Corps.

The engineers had barely finished ascertaining this much when it became urgent to abandon ship. They would soon strike atmosphere. That would complete the ruin of the hull. Struggling through airlessness, weightlessness, lightlessness, hale survivors dragged hurt to the boat housing. There wasn't room for all those bodies if they stayed space armored. Flandry pressurized from tanks and, as each man cycled through the airlock, had his bulky gear stripped off and sent out the disposal valve. He managed to find stowage for three suits; including his—which he suddenly remembered he must not wear when everyone else would be unprotected. That was more for the sake of the impellers secured to them than for anything else.

Those worst injured were placed in the safety-webbed chairs. The rest, jammed together down the aisle, would depend for their lives on the gee-field. Flandry saw Kathryn take her stand among them. He wanted wildly to give her the copilot's chair; the field circuits might well be disrupted by the stresses they were about to encounter. But Ensign Havelock had some training in this kind of emergency procedure. His help could be the critical quantum that saved her.

A shudder went through boat and bones, the first impact on Dido's stratosphere. Flandry shot free.

The rest was indescribable: riding a meteorite through incandescence, shock, thunderblast, stormwind, night, mountains and caverns of cloud, rain like bullets, crazy tilting and whirling of horribly onrushing horizon, while the noise roared and battered and vibrations shook brains in skulls and devils danced on the instrument panel.

Somehow Flandry and Havelock kept a measure of control. They braked the worst of their velocity before they got down to altitudes where it would be fatal. They did not skip helplessly off the tropopause nor flip and tumble when they crossed high winds in the lower atmosphere. They avoided peaks that raked up to catch them and a monstrous hurricane, violent beyond anything. Terra had ever known, that would have sundered their boat and cast it into the sea. Amidst the straining over meters and displays, the frantic leap of hands over pilot board and feet on pedals, the incessant brutality of sound, heat, throbbing, they clung to awareness of their location.

Their desire was wholly to reach Port Frederiksen. Their descent took them around the northern hemisphere. Identifying what had to be the largest continent, they fought their way to the approximately correct latitude and slanted down westward above it.

They could have made their goal, or come near, had their initial velocity been in the right direction. But the instrumental survey had been expedited by throwing *Asieneuve* into a retrograde orbit. Now the planet's rotation worked against them, forcing extra energy expenditure in the early stages of deceleration. By the time the boat was approaching a safe speed, its accumulators were drained. Overloaded, it had no possibility of a long ballistic glide. There was nothing to do but use the last stored joules for setting down.

Nor could the tail jacks be employed. Unharnessed, men would be crushed beneath their fellows if the gee-field gave way. Flandry picked out an open area surrounded by forest. Water gleamed between hummocks and sedgy clumps. Better marsh than treetops. The keel skids hissed beneath a last rumble of engine; the boat rocked, bucked, slewed around, and came to rest at a steep angle; flying creatures fled upward in clamorous thousands; and stillness was.

A moment's dark descended on Flandry. He pulled out of it to the sound of feeble cheers. "E-e-everybody all right?" he stuttered. His fingers trembled likewise, fumbling with his harness.

"No further injuries, sir," said one voice.

"Maybe not," another responded. "But O'Brien died on the way down."

Flandry closed his eyes. *My man, pierced him. My men. My ship. How many are left? I counted. . . . Twenty-three with only small hurts, plus Kathryn and me. Seventeen—sixteen—seriously wounded. The rest—Those lives were in my hands!*

Havelock said diffidently, "Our radio's out, sir. We can't call for help. What does the captain wish?"

Rovian, I should have collected that chunk, not you. The lives that are left are still in my murderous-clumsy hands.

Flandry forced his lids back up. His ears were ringing almost too loudly for him to hear his own words, but he thought they sounded mechanical. "We can't maintain our interior field long. The final ergs are about to go. Let's get our casualties outside before we have to contend with local pull on a slanted deck." He rose and faced his men. Never had he done anything harder. "Lady McCormac," he said. "You know this planet. Have you any recommendations?"

She was hidden from him by those packed around her. The husky tones were unshaken. "Equalize pressures slowly. If we're anywhere near sea level, that air is half again as thick as Terran. Do you know where we are?"

"We were aiming for the Aenean base."

"If I remember rightly, this hemisphere's in its early summer. S'posin' we're not far below the arctic circle, we'll have more day than night, but not very much more. Bear in mind the short spin period. Don't count on a lot of light."

"Thanks." Flandry issued the obvious commands.

Saavedra, the communications officer, found some tools, took the panel off the radio transceiver, and studied it. "I might be able to cobble something together for signalling the base," he said.

"How long'll that take you?" Flandry asked. A little potency was returning to his muscles, a little clarity to his brain.

"Several hours, sir. I'll have to haywire, and jigger around till I'm on a standard band."

"And maybe nobody'll happen to be listening. And when they do hear us, they'll have to triangulate and—Uh-uh." Flandry shook his head. "We can't wait. Another ship's on her way here. When she finds the derelict we shot up, she'll hunt for us. An excellent chance of finding us, too: a sweep with metal detectors over a planet as primitive as this. I don't want us anywhere near. She's likely to throw a missile."

"What shall we do, then, sir?" Havelock asked.

"Does my lady think we've a chance of marching overland to the base?" Flandry called.

"Depends on just where we are," Kathryn replied. "Topography, native cultures, everything's as variable on Dido as 'tis on most worlds. Can we pack plenty of food?"

"Yes, I imagine so. Boats like this are stocked with ample freeze-dried rations. I assume there's plenty of safe water."

"Is. Might be stinkin' and scummy, but no Didonian bug has yet made a human sick. Biochemistry's that different."

When the lock was opened full, the air turned into a steam bath. Odors blew strange, a hundred pungencies, fragrant, sharp, rotten, spicy, nameless. Men gasped and tried to sweat. One rating started to pull off his shirt. Kathryn laid a hand on his arm. "Don't," she warned. "No matter clouds, enough UV gets past to burn you."

Flandry went first down the accommodation ladder. Weight was hardly changed. He identified a tinge of ozone in the swamp reeks and thought that an increased partial pressure of oxygen might prove valuable. His boots squelched into ankle-deep muck. The sounds of life were coming back: chatter, caw, whistle, wingbeats. They were loud in the dense air, now that his hearing had recovered. Small animals flitted among leaves in the jungle.

It was not like a rain forest on a really terrestroid world. The variety of trees was incredible, from gnarly and thorny dwarfs to soaring slim giants. Vines and fungoids covered many dark trunks. Foliage was equally diverse in its shapes. Nowhere was it green; browns and deep reds predominated, though purples and golds blent in; the same held for the spongy, springy mat on the land. The overall effect was one of somber richness. There were no real shadows, but Flandry's gaze soon lost itself in the gloom under the trees. He saw more brush than he liked to think about pushing his way through.

Overhead the sky was pearl gray. Lower cloud strata drifted across its featurelessness. A vaguely luminous area marked Virgil. Recalling where the terminator was, he knew this district was still at morning. They'd leave before sundown if they worked.

He gave himself to helping. The labor was hard. For that he was grateful. It rescued him from dead men and a wrecked ship.

First the wounded must be borne to higher, drier ground.

71

Their injuries were chiefly broken bones and concussions. If your armor was ripped open in space, that was generally the end of you. Two men did have nasty abdominal gashes from bits of metal whose entry holes had been sufficiently small for them or friends to slap on patches before their air could flee them. One man was unconscious, skin chill, breath shallow, pulse thready. And O'Brien had died.

Luckily, the medical officer was on his feet. He got busy. Arriving with an armful of equipment, Flandry saw Kathryn giving him skilled assistance. He remembered in dull surprise that she'd disappeared for a while. It didn't seem like her not to plunge straight into a task.

By the time the last item had been unloaded, she had finished her nurse's job and supervised a burial party. He glimpsed her doing some of the digging herself. When he slogged to her, O'Brien was laid out in the grave. Water oozed upward around him. He had no coffin. She had covered him with the Imperial flag.

"Will the captain read the service?" she asked.

He looked at her. She was as muddy and exhausted as he, but stood straight. Her hair clung wet to head and cheeks, but was the sole brightness upon this world. Sheathed on a belt around her coverall, he recognized the great blade and knuckleduster half of his Merseian war knife.

Stupid from weariness, he blurted, "Do *you* want me to?"

"He wasn't the enemy," she said. "He was of Hugh's people. Give him his honor."

She handed him the prayerbook. *Me?* he thought. *But I never believed—* She was watching. They all were. His fingers stained the pages as he read aloud the majestic words. A fine drizzle began.

While trenching tools clinked, Kathryn plucked Flandry's sleeve. "A minute, of your courtesy," she said. They walked aside. "I spent a while scoutin' 'round," she told him. "Studied the vegetation, climbed a tree and saw mountains to west —and you wouldn't spy many pteropods at this season if we were east of the Stonewall, so the range ahead of us must be the Maurusian—well, I know roughly where we are."

His heart skipped a beat. "And something about the territory?"

"Less'n I'd wish. My work was mainly in Gaetulia. However, I did have my first season in this general area, more for trainin' than research. Point is, we've got a fair chance of findin' Didonians that've met humans; and the local culture is reasonably high; and if we do come on an entity that knows one of our pidgins, it'll be a version I can talk, and I should be able to understand their lingo after a little practice." The black brows knitted. "I'll not hide from you, better if we'd come down west of the Maurusians, and not just 'cause that'd shorten our march. They have some wild and mean dwellers. However, maybe I can bargain for an escort to the other side."

"Good. You didn't perchance find a trail for us?"

"Why, yes. That's what I was mainly searchin' for. We wouldn't make a kilometer 'fore sundown through muscoid and arrowbush, not if we exhausted our blasters burnin' them. I've found one just a few meters from the swamp edge, aimed more or less our way."

"Sizzle it," Flandry said, "but I wish we were on the same side, you and I!"

"We are," she smiled. "What can you do but surrender at Port Frederiksen?"

His failure rose in him, tasting of vomit. "Doubtless nothing. Let's get loaded and start." He turned on his heel and left her, but could not escape the look that followed him. It burned between his shoulderblades.

The stuff from the boat weighed heavily on men who must also take turns carrying the wounded on improvised stretchers. Besides food, changes of clothing, utensils, hand guns, ammunition, ripped-off plastic sheeting for shelters, and other necessities, Flandry insisted on taking the three spacesuits. Havelock ventured to protest: "If the captain please, should we lug them? The impellers could be handy for sendin' scouts aloft, but they aren't good for many kilometers in planet gravity, nor will their radios reach far. And I don't imagine we'll meet any critters that we have to wear armor to fight."

"We may have to discard things," Flandry admitted, "but I'm hoping for native porters. We'll tote the suits a ways, at least."

"Sir, the men are dead on their feet as is!"

Flandry stared into the blond young face. "Would you rather be dead on your back?" he snapped. His eyes traversed the weary, dirty, stoop-shouldered creatures for whom he was responsible. "Saddle up," he said. "Lend me a hand, Citizen Havelock. I don't intend to carry less than anybody else."

A sighing went among them through the thin sad rain, but they obeyed.

The trail proved a blessing. Twigs and gravel mixed into its dirt—by Didonians, Kathryn said—gave a hard broad surface winding gradually through inwalling forest toward higher country.

Dusk fell, layer by layer. Flandry made the group continue, with flashbeams to show the way. He pretended not to hear the *sotto voce* remarks behind his back, though they hurt. Night fell, scarcely cooler than day, tomb black, full of croakings and distant cries, while the men lurched on.

After another nightmare hour, Flandry called a halt. A brook ran across the trail. High trees surrounded and roofed a tiny meadow. His light flew about, bringing leaves and eyes briefly out of murk. "Water and camouflage," he said. "What do you think, my lady?"

"Good," she said.

"You see," he tried to explain, "we have to rest, and daybreak will be soon. I don't want us observed from the air."

She didn't reply. *I rate no answer, who lost my ship,* he thought.

Men eased off their burdens. A few munched food bars before collapsing into sleep with their fellows. The medical officer, Felipe Kapunan, said to Flandry, "No doubt the captain feels he should take first watch. But I'll be busy the next hour or two, seeing to my patients. Dressings need change, they could use fresh enzymes, anti-radiation shots, pain killers—the standard stuff, no help necessary. You may as well rest, sir. I'll call you when I finish."

His last sentence was scarcely heard. Flandry went down and down into miraculous nothingness. His last knowledge was that the ground cover—carpet weed, Kathryn named it, despite its being more suggestive of miniature red-brown sponges—made a damp but otherwise gentle mattress.

The doctor shook him awake as promised and offered him a stimpill. Flandry gulped it. Coffee would have been welcome, but he dared not yet allow a campfire. He circled the meadow, found a seat between two enormous roots, and relaxed with his back against the bole. The rain had paused.

Dawn was stealthy on Dido. Light seemed to condense in the hot rank air, drop by drop, like the mists whose tendrils crawled across the sleepers. Except for the clucking brook and drip of water off leaves, a great silence had fallen.

A footstep broke it. Flandry started to rise, his blaster half out of the sheath. When he saw her, he holstered the weapon and bowed around his shivering heart. "My lady. What . . . what has you awake this early?"

"Couldn't sleep. Too much to think 'bout. Mind if I join you?"

"How could I?"

They sat down together. He contrived his position so that

it was natural to watch her. She looked into the jungle for a space. Exhaustion smudged her eyes and paled her lips.

Abruptly she faced back to him. "Talk with me, Dominic Flandry," she pleaded. "I think 'bout Hugh . . . now I can hope to meet him again. . . . Can I stay with him? Wouldn't there always be that between us?"

"I said," *a cosmic cycle ago,* "that if he'd, well, let a girl like you get away from him, for any cause, he's an idiot."

"Thanks." She reached across and squeezed his hand. He felt the touch for a long while afterward. "Shall we be friends? First-name friends?"

"I'd love that."

"We should make a little ceremony of it, in the Aenean way." Her smile was wistful. "Drink a toast and— But later, Dominic, later." She hesitated. "The war's over for you, after all. You'll be interned. No prison; a room in Nova Roma ought to do. I'll come visit when I can, bring Hugh when he's free. Maybe we'll talk you into joinin' us. I do wish so."

"First we'd better reach Port Frederiksen," he said, not daring anything less banal.

"Yes." She leaned forward. "Let's discuss that. I told you I need conversation. Poor Dominic, you save me from captivity, then from death, now 'tis got to be from my personal horrors. Please talk practical."

He met the green eyes in the wide strong face. "Well," he said, "this is quite a freakish planet, isn't it?"

She nodded. "They think it started out to be Venus type, but a giant asteroid collided with it. Shock waves blew most of the atmosphere off, leavin' the rest thin enough that chemical evolution could go on, not too unlike the Terran—photosynthesis and so forth, though the amino acids that developed happened to be mainly dextro- 'stead of levorotatory. Same collision must've produced the extreme axial tilt, and maybe the high rotation. 'Cause of those factors, the oceans aren't as inert as you might 'spect on a moonless world, and storms are fierce. Lot of tectonic activity: no s'prise, is it? That's believed to be the reason we don't find traces of past ice ages, but do find eras of abnormal heat and drought. Nobody knows for sure, though. In thousands of man-lifetimes, we've barely won a glimpse into the mysteries. This is a whole *world,* Dominic."

"I understand that," he said. "Uh, any humanly comfortable areas?"

"Not many. Too hot and wet. Some high and polar regions aren't as bad as this, and Port Frederiksen enjoys winds off a cold current. The tropics kill you in a few days if you're not protected. No, we don't want this planet for our-selves, only for knowledge: It belongs to the autochthons any-way." Her mood turned suddenly defiant: "When Hugh's Emperor, he'll see that all autochthons get a fair break."

"If he ever is." It was as if someone else sat down at a control console in Flandry's brain and made him say, "Why did he bring in barbarians?"

"He must've gone elsewhere himself and needed them to guard Virgil." She looked aside. "I asked a couple of your men who'd watched on viewscreens, what that ship was like. 'Twas Darthan, from their descriptions. Not truly hostile folk."

"As long as they aren't given the chance to be! We'd offered Pax, and nevertheless they fired."

"They . . . well, Darthans often act like that. Their culture makes it hard for them to believe a call for truce is honest. Hugh had to take what he could get in a hurry. After every-thing that'd happened, what reason had he to tell them some-one might come for parley? He's mortal! He can't think of everything!"

Flandry slumped. "I suppose not, my lady."

A fluting went through the forest. Kathryn waited a minute before she said gently, "You know, you haven't yet spoken my right name."

He replied in his emptiness: "How can I? Men are gone because of what I did."

"Oh, Dominic!" The tears broke forth out of her. He fought to hold back his own.

They found themselves kneeling together, his face hidden against her breasts, his arms around her waist and her left around his neck, her right hand smoothing his hair while he shuddered.

"Dominic, Dominic," she whispered to him, "I know. How well I know. My man's a captain too. More ships, more lives than you could count. How often I've seen him readin' cas-ualty reports! I'll tell you, he's come to me and closed the door so he could weep. He's made his errors that killed men. What commander hasn't? But somebody's got to command. It's your duty. You weigh the facts best's you're able, and de-cide, and act, and long's you did do your best, you never look back. You needn't. You mustn't.

"Dominic, we didn't make this carnivore universe. We only live here, and have to try and cope.

"Who said you were in error? Your estimate was com-pletely reasonable. I don't believe any board of inquiry 'ud blame you. If Hugh couldn't foresee you'd come with me, how could you foresee—? Dominic, look up, be glad again."

A moment's hell-colored light struck through the eastern leaves. Seconds after, the air roared and a queasy vibration moved the ground.

Men stumbled to their feet. Flandry and Kathryn bounded apart. "What's that?" cried Saavedra.

"That," Flandry yelled into the wind that had arisen, "was the second barbarian ship making sure of our boat."

A minute later they heard the ongoing thunderclap of a large body traveling at supersonic speed. It faded into a terrible whistle and was gone. The gust died out and startled flying creatures circled noisily back toward their trees.

"High-yield warhead," Flandry judged. "They meant to kill within several kilometers' radius." He held a wet finger to the normal dawn breeze. "The fallout's bound east; we needn't worry. I'm stonkerish glad we hiked this far yesterday!"

Kathryn took both his hands. "Your doin' alone, Dominic," she said. "Will that stop your grief?"

It didn't, really. But she had given him the courage to think: *Very well. Nothing's accomplished by these idealistic broodings. Dead's dead. My job is to salvage the living . . . and afterward, if there is an afterward, use whatever tricks I can to prevent my superiors from blaming me too severely.*

No doubt my conscience will. But maybe I can learn how to jettison it. An officer of the Empire is much more efficient without one.

"At ease, men," he said. "We'll spend the next rotation period here, recuperating, before we push on."

IX

The forest opened abruptly on cleared land. Stepping out, Flandry saw ordered rows of bushes. On three sides the farm was hemmed in by jungle, on the fourth it dropped into a valley full of vapors. The trend of his six Didonian days of travel had been upward.

He didn't notice the agriculture at once. "Hold!" he barked. The blaster jumped into his grasp. *A rhinoceros herd?*

No . . . not really . . . of course not. Lord Advisor Mulele's African preserve lay 200 light-years remote. The half-dozen animals before him had the size and general build of rhinos, though their nearly hairless slate-blue skins were smooth rather than wrinkled and tails were lacking. But the shoulders of each protruded sidewise to make a virtual platform. The ears were big and fanlike. The skull bulged high above a pair of beady eyes, supported a horn on the nose, then tapered to a muzzle whose mouth was oddly soft and flexible. The horn offset that effect by being a great ebony blade with a sawtoothed ridge behind it.

"Wait, Dominic!" Kathryn sped to join him. "Don't shoot. Those're nogas."

"Hm?" He lowered the gun.

"Our word. Humans can't pronounce any Didonian language."

"You mean they are the—" Flandry had encountered curious forms of sophont, but none without some equivalent of hands. What value would an intelligence have that could not actively reshape its environment?

Peering closer, he saw that the beasts were not at graze. Two knelt in a corner of the field, grubbing stumps, while a

78

third rolled a trimmed log toward a building whose roof was visible over a hillcrest. The fourth dragged a crude wooden plow across the newly acquired ground. The fifth came behind, its harness enabling it to steer. A pair of smaller animals rode on its shoulders. That area was some distance off, details hard to make out through the hazy air. The sixth, nearer to Flandry, was not feeding so much as removing weeds from among the bushes.

"C'mon!" Kathryn dashed ahead, lightfoot under her pack.

The trip had been day-and-night trudgery. In camp, he and she had been too occupied—the only ones with wilderness experience—for any meaningful talk before they must sleep. But they were rewarded; unable to mourn, they began to mend. Now eagerness made her suddenly so vivid that Flandry lost consciousness of his surroundings. She became everything he could know, like a nearby sun.

"Halloo!" She stopped and waved her arms.

The nogas halted too and squinted nearsightedly. Their ears and noses twitched, straining into the rank dank heat. Flandry was jolted back to the world. They could attack her. "Deploy," he rapped at those of his men who carried weapons. "Half circle behind me. The rest of you stand at the trailhead." He ran to Kathryn's side.

Wings beat. A creature that had been hovering, barely visible amidst low clouds, dropped straight toward the sixth noga. "A kríppo." Kathryn seized Flandry's hand. "I wish I could've told you in advance. But watch. 'Tis wonderful."

The nogas were presumably more or less mammalian, also in their reproductive pattern: the sexes were obvious, the females had udders. The krippo resembled a bird . . . did it? The body was comparable to that of a large goose, with feathers gray-brown above, pale gray below, tipped with blue around the throat, on the pinions, at the end of a long triangular tail. The claws were strong, meant to grab and hang on. The neck was fairly long itself, supporting a head that swelled grotesquely backward. The face seemed to consist mainly of two great topaz eyes. And there was no beak, only a red cartilaginous tube.

The krippo landed on the noga's right shoulder. It thrust a ropy tongue (?) from the tube. Flandry noticed a knot on either side of the noga, just below the platform. The right one uncoiled, revealing itself to be a member suggestive of a tentacle, more than two meters in length if fully outstretched. The krippo's extended equivalent, the "tongue," plunged into a sphincter at the end of this. Linked, the two organisms trotted toward the humans.

79

"We're still lackin' a ruka," Kathryn said. "No, wait." The noga behind the plow had bellowed. "That entity's callin' for one. Heesh's own ruka has to unharness heesh 'fore heesh can come to us."

"But the rest—" Flandry pointed. Four nogas merely stood where they were.

"Sure," Kathryn said. "Without partners, they're dumb brutes. They won't act, 'cept for the kind of rote job they were doin', till they get a signal from a complete entity. . . . Ah. Here we go."

A new animal dropped from a tree and scampered over the furrows. It was less analogous to an ape than the noga was to a rhinoceros or the krippo to a bird. However, a Terran was bound to think of it in such terms. About a meter tall if it stood erect, it must use its short, bowed legs arboreally by choice, for it ran on all fours and either foot terminated in three well-developed grasping digits. The tail was prehensile. The chest, shoulders, and arms were enormous in proportion, greater than a man's; and besides three fingers, each hand possessed a true thumb. The head was similarly massive, round, with bowl-shaped ears and luminous brown eyes. Like the krippo, this creature had no nose or mouth, simply a nostrilled tube. Black hair covered it, except where ears, extremities, and a throat pouch showed blue skin. It—he—was male. He wore a belt supporting a purse and an iron dagger.

"Is that a Didonian?" Flandry asked.

"A ruka," Kathryn said. "One-third of a Dodonian."

The animal reached the noga closest to the humans. He bounded onto the left shoulder, settled down by the krippo, and thrust out a "tongue" of his own to join the remaining "tentacle."

"You see," Kathryn said hurriedly, "we had to name them somehow. In most Didonian languages, the species are called things answerin' roughly to 'feet,' 'wings,' and 'hands.' But that'd get confusin' in Anglic. So, long's Aenean dialects contain some Russko anyhow, we settled on 'noga,' 'krippo,' 'ruka.' " The tripartite being stopped a few meters off. "Rest your gun. Heesh won't hurt us."

She went to meet it. Flandry followed, a bit dazed. Symbiotic relationships were not unknown to him. The most spectacular case he'd met hitherto was among the Togru-Kon-Tanakh of Vanrijn. A gorilloid supplied hands and strength; a small, carapaced partner had brains and keen eyes; the detachable organs that linked them contained cells for joining the two nervous systems into one. Apparently evolution on Dido had gone the same way.

But off the deep end! Flandry thought. *To the point where the two little types no longer even eat, but draw blood off the big one. Lord, how horrible. Never to revel in a tournedos or a pêche flambée—*

He and Kathryn stopped before the autochthon. A horsey aroma, not unpleasant, wafted down a light, barely cooling breeze. Flandry wondered which pair of eyes to meet.

The noga grunted. The krippo trilled through its nostrils, which must have some kind of strings and resonating chamber. The ruka inflated his throat pouch and produced a surprising variety of sounds.

Kathryn listened intently. "I'm no expert in this language," she said, "but they do speak a related one 'round Port Frederiksen, so I can follow 'long fairly well. Heesh's name is Master Of Songs, though 'name' has the wrong connotations. . . ." She uttered vocables. Flandry caught a few Anglic words, but couldn't really understand her.

I suppose all Didonians are too alien to learn a human tongue, he thought. *The xenologists must have worked out different pidgins for the different linguistic families: noises that a Terran epiglottis can wrap itself around, on a semantic pattern that a Didonian can comprehend.* He regarded Kathryn with renewed marveling. *What brains that must have taken!*

Three voices answered her. *The impossibility of a human talking a Didonian language can't just be a matter of larynx and mouth,* Flandry realized. *A vocalizer would deal with that. No, the structure's doubtless contrapuntal.*

"Heesh doesn't know pidgin," Kathryn told him. "But Cave Discoverer does. They'll assemble heesh for us."

"Heesh?"

She chuckled. "What pronoun's right, in a situation like this? A few cultures insist on some particular sex distribution in the units of an entity. But for most, sex isn't what matters, 'tis the species and individual capabilities of the units, and they form entities in whatever combinations seem best at a given time. So we call a partnership, whether complete or two-way, 'heesh.' And we don't fool 'round inflectin' the word."

The krippo took off in a racket of wings. The ruka stayed aboard the noga. But it was as if a light had dimmed. The two stared at the humans a while, then the ruka scratched himself and the noga began cropping weeds.

"You need all three for full intelligence," Flandry deduced.

Kathryn nodded. "M-hm. The rukas have the most forebrain. Alone, one of them is 'bout equal to a chimpanzee. Is that right, the smartest Terran subhuman? And the noga

81

alone is pretty stupid. A three-way, though, can think as well as you or I. Maybe better, if comparison's possible. We're still tryin' to find tests and measurements that make sense." She frowned. "Do have the boys put away their guns. We're 'mong good people."

Flandry acceded, but left his followers posted where they were. If anything went agley, he wanted that trail held. The hurt men lay there on their stretchers.

The other partnership finished disengaging itself—no, heeshself—from the plow. The earth thudded to the gallop of heesh's noga; krippo and ruka must be hanging on tight! Kathryn addressed this Didonian when heesh arrived, also without result though she did get a response. This she translated as: "Meet Skilled With Soil, who knows of our race even if none of heesh's units have learned pidgin."

Flandry rubbed his chin. His last application of antibeard enzyme was still keeping it smooth, but he lamented the scraggly walrus effect that his mustache was sprouting. "I take it," he said, "that invidi—uh, units swap around to form, uh, entities whose natural endowment is optimum for whatever is to be done?"

"Yes. In most cultures we've studied. Skilled With Soil is evidently just what the phrase implies, a gifted farmer. In other combinations, heesh's units might be part of an outstandin' hunter or artisan or musician or whatever. That's why there's no requirement for a large population in order to have a variety of specialists within a communion."

"Did you say 'communion'?"

"Seems more accurate than 'community,' true?"

"But why doesn't everybody know what anybody does?"

"Well, learnin' does seem to go easier'n for our race, but 'tis not instantaneous. Memory traces have to be reinforced if they're not to fade out; skills have to be developed through practice. And, natur'ly, a brain holds the *kind* of memories and skills 'tis equipped to hold. For instance, nogas keep the botanical knowledge, 'cause they do the eatin'; rukas, havin' hands, remember the manual trades; krippos store meteorological and geographical data. 'Tis not quite that simple, really. All species store some information of every sort—we think—'speci'ly language. But you get the idea, I'm sure."

"Nonetheless—"

"Let me continue, Dominic." Enthusiasm sparkled from Kathryn as Flandry had never seen it from a woman before. "Question of culture. Didonian societies vary as much as ever Terran ones did. Certain cultures let entities form promiscuously. The result is, units learn less from others than they

82

might, for lack of concentrated attention; emotional and intellectual life is shallow; the group stays at a low level of savagery. Certain other cultures are 'stremely restrictive 'bout relationships. For 'sample, the units of an entity are often s'posed to belong to each other 'sclusively till death do them part, 'cept for a grugin' temporary linkage with immature ones as a necessity of education. Those societies tend to be further along technologically, but nowhere beyond the stone age and everywhere esthetically impoverished. In neither case are the Didonians realizin' their full potential."

"I see," Flandry drawled. "Playboys versus puritans."

She blinked, then grinned. "As you will. Anyhow, most cultures—like this one, clearly—do it right. Every unit belongs to a few stable entities, dividin' time roughly equally 'mong them. That way, these entities develop true personalities, broadly backgrounded but each with a maximum talent in heesh's specialty. In addition, less developed partnerships are assembled temporarily at need."

She glanced skyward. "I think Cave Discoverer's 'bout to be created for us," she said.

Two krippos circled down. One presumably belonged to Master Of Songs, the other to Cave Discoverer, though Flandry couldn't tell them apart. Master Of Songs and Cave Discoverer apparently had a noga and ruka in common.

The bird shape in the lead took stance on the platform. The companion flew off to find a noga for itself. More krippos were appearing over the trees, more rukas scampering from the woods or the house. *We'll have a regular town meeting here in a minute,* Flandry anticipated.

He directed his awareness back to Kathryn and Cave Discoverer. A dialogue had commenced between them. It went haltingly at first, neither party having encountered pidgin for some years and the language of this neighborhood not being precisely identical with that which was spoken around Port Frederiksen. After a while, discourse gained momentum.

The rest of the communion arrived to watch, listen, and have the talk interpreted for them—aside from those who were out hunting or gathering, as Flandry learned later. An entity moved close to him. The ruka sprang off and approached, trailing the noga's thick "umbilicus" across a shoulder. Blue fingers plucked at Flandry's clothes and tried to unsheath his blaster for examination. The man didn't want to allow that, even if he put the weapon on safety, but Kathryn might disapprove of outright refusal. Removing his homemade packsack, he spread its contents on the ground. That served to keep the rukas of several curious entities occupied.

83

After he saw they were not stealing or damaging, Flandry sat down and let his mind wander until it got to Kathryn. There it stayed.

An hour or so had passed, the brief day was drawing to a close, when she summoned him with a wave. "They're glad to meet us, willin' to offer hospitality," she said, "but dubious 'bout helpin' us across the mountains. The dwellers yonder are dangerous. Also, this is a busy season in the forest as well as the plowland. At the same time, the communion 'ud surely like the payment I promise, things like firearms and proper steel tools. They'll create one they call Many Thoughts and let heesh ponder the question. Meanwhile we're invited to stay."

Lieutenant Kapunan was especially pleased with that. Such medicines as he had were keeping his patients from getting worse, but the stress of travel hadn't let them improve much. If he could remain here with them while the rest went after help—Flandry agreed. The march might produce casualties of its own, but if so, they ought to be fewer.

Everyone took off for the house. The humans felt dwarfed by the lumbering bulks around them: all but Kathryn. She laughed and chattered the whole way. "Kind of a home-comin' for me, this," she told her companions. "I'd 'most forgotten how 'scitin' 'tis, field work on Dido, and how I, well, yes, love them."

You have a lot of capacity to love, Flandry thought. He recognized it as a pleasing remark that he would have used on any other girl; but he felt shy about flattering this one.

When they topped the ridge, they had a view of the farther slope. It dropped a way, then rose again, forming a shelter for the dwelling place. Artificial channels, feeding into a stream, must prevent flooding. In the distance, above trees, a bare crag loomed athwart the clouds. Thence came the rumble of a major waterfall. Kathryn pointed. "They call this region Thunderstone," she said, " 'mong other things. Places come closer to havin' true names than entities do."

The homestead consisted of turf-roofed log buildings and a rude corral, enclosing a yard cobbled agianst the frequent mudmaking rains. Most of the structures were sheds and cribs. The biggest was the longhouse, impressive in workmanship and carved ornamentation as well as sheer size. Flandry paid more heed at first to the corral. Juveniles of all three species occupied it, together with four adults of each kind. The grownups formed pairs in different combinations, with immature third units. Other young wandered about, dozed, or took nourishment. The cows nursed the noga calves—two

84

adults were lactating females, one was dry, one was male—
and were in turn tapped by fuzzy little rukas and fledgling krippos.

"School?" Flandry asked.

"You might say so," Kathryn answered. "Primary stages of
learnin' and development. Too important to interrupt for us;
not that a partial entity 'ud care anyway. While they grow,
the young'll partner 'mong themselves also. But in the end, as
a rule, they'll replace units that've died out of established entities."

"Heh! 'If youth knew, if age could.' The Didonians appear to have solved that problem."

"And conquered death, in a way. 'Course, over several
generations, a given personality 'ull fade into an altogether
new one, and most of the earlier memories 'ull be lost. Still,
the continuity—D' you see why they fascinate us?"

"Indeed. I haven't the temperament for being a scientist,
but you make me wish I did."

She regarded him seriously. "In your fashion, Dominic,
you're as much a filosof as anybody I've known."

My men are a gallant crew, he thought, *and they're enti-
tled to my loyalty as well as my leadership, but at the moment I'd prefer them and their big flapping ears ten parsecs
hence.*

The doors and window shutters of the lodge stood open,
making its interior more bright and cool than he had awaited.
The floor was fire-hardened clay strewn with fresh boughs.
Fantastically carved pillars and rafters upheld the roof. The
walls were hung with skins, crudely woven tapestries, tools,
weapons, and objects that Kathryn guessed were sacred. Built
in along them were stalls for nogas, perches for krippos,
benches for rukas. Above were sconced torches for night illu-
mination. Fires burned in pits; hoods, of leather stretched on
wooden frames, helped draw smoke out through ventholes.
Cubs, calves, and chicks, too small for education, bumbled
about like the pet animals they were. Units that must be too
aged or ill for daily toil waited quietly near the middle of the
house. It was all one enormous room. Privacy was surely an
idea which Didonians were literally incapable of entertaining.
But what ideas did they have that were forever beyond
human reach?

Flandry gestured at a pelt. "If they're herbivorous, the big
chaps, I mean, why do they hunt?" he wondered.

"Animal products," Kathryn said. "Leather, bone, sinew,
grease . . . sh!"

The procession drew up before a perch whereon sat an old

85

krippo. Gaunt, lame in one wing, he nevertheless reminded Flandry of eagles. Every noga lowered the horn to him. The flyer belonging to Cave Discoverer let go and flapped off to a place of his (?) own. That noga offered his vacated tentacle. The ancient made union. His eyes turned on the humans and fairly blazed.

"Many Thoughts," Kathryn whispered to Flandry. "Their wisest. Heesh'll take a minute to absorb what the units can convey."

"Do that fowl's partners belong to every prominent citizen?"

"Sh, not so loud. I don't know local customs, but they seem to have special respect for Many Thoughts. . . . Well, you'd 'spect the units with the best genetic heritage to be in the best entities, wouldn't you? I gather Cave Discoverer's an explorer and adventurer. Heesh first met humans by seekin' out a xenological camp 200 kilometers from here. Many Thoughts gets .the vigor and boldness of the same noga and ruka, but heesh's own journeys are of the spirit. . . . Ah, I think heesh's ready now. I'll have to repeat whatever information went away with the former krippo."

That conversation lasted beyond nightfall. The torches were lit, the fires stoked, cooking begun in stone pots. While the nogas could live on raw vegetation, they preferred more concentrated and tasty food when they could get it. A few more Didonians came home from the woods, lighting their way with luminous fungoids. They carried basketsful of edible roots. No doubt hunters and foragers remained out for a good many days at a stretch. The lodge filled with droning, fluting, coughing talk. Flandry and his men had trouble fending curiosity seekers off their injured without acting unfriendly.

At last Kathryn made the best imitation she could of the gesture of deference, and sought out her fellow humans. In the leaping red light, her eyes and locks stood brilliant among shadows. " 'Twasn't easy," she said in exuberance, 'but I argued heesh into it. We'll have an escort—mighty small, but an escort, guides and porters. I reckon we can start in another forty-fifty hours . . . for home!"

"Your home," growled a man.

"Dog your hatch," Flandry ordered him.

X

Centuries before, a rogue planet had passed near Beta Crucis. Sunless worlds are not uncommon, but in astronomical immensity it is rare for one to encounter a star. This globe swung by and receded on a hyperbolic orbit. Approximately Terra-size, it had outgassed vapors in the ardor of its youth. Then, as internal heat radiated away, atmosphere froze. The great blue sun melted the oceans and boiled the air back into fluidity. For some years, appalling violence reigned.

Eventually interstellar cold would have reclaimed its dominion, and the incident would have had no significance. But chance ordained that the passage occur in the old bold days of the Polesotechnic League, and that it be noticed by those who saw an incalculable fortune to be won. Isotope synthesis on the scale demanded by a starfaring civilization had been industry's worst bottleneck. Seas and skies were needed for coolants, continents for dumping of radioactive wastes. Every lifeless body known had been too frigid or too hot or otherwise unsuitable. But here came Satan, warmed to an ideal temperature which the heat of nuclear manufacture could maintain. As soon as the storms and quakes had abated, the planet was swarmed by entrepreneurs.

During the Troubles, ownership, legal status, input and output, every aspect of relationship to the living fraction of the universe, varied as wildly for Satan as for most worlds. For a while it was abandoned. But no one had ever actually dwelt there. No being could survive that poisonous air and murderous radiation background, unless for the briefest of visits with the heaviest of protection. Robots, computers, and automatons were the inhabitants. They continued operating

87

while civilization fragmented, fought, and somewhat reconstructed itself. When at last an Imperial aristocrat sent down a self-piloting freighter, they loaded it from a dragon's hoard.

The defense of Satan became a major reason to garrison and colonize Sector Alpha Crucis.

Its disc hung darkling among the stars in a viewscreen of Hugh McCormac's command room. Beta had long since dwindled to merely the brightest of them, and the machines had scant need for visible light. You saw the sphere blurred by gas, a vague shimmer of clouds and oceans, blacknesses that were land. It was a desolate scene, the more so when you called up an image of the surface—raw mountains, gashed valleys, naked stone plains, chill and stagnant seas, all cloaked in a night relieved only by a rare lamp or an evil blue glow of fluorescence, no sound but a dreary wind-skirl or a rushing of forever sterile waters, no happening throughout its eons but the inanimate, unaware toil of the machines.

For Hugh McCormac, though, Satan meant victory.

He took his gaze from the planet and let it stray in the opposite direction, toward open sapce. Men were dying where those constellations glittered. "I should be yonder," he said. "I should have insisted."

"You couldn't do anything, sir," Edgar Oliphant told him. "Once the tactical dispositions are made, the game plays itself. And you might be killed."

"That's what's wrong." McCormac twisted his fingers together. "Here we are, snug and safe in orbit, while a battle goes on to make *me* Emperor!"

"You're the High Admiral too, sir." A cigar in Oliphant's mouth wagged and fumed as he talked. "You've got to be available where the data flow in, to make decisions in case anything unpredicted happens."

"I know, I know." McCormac strode back and forth, from end to end of the balcony on which they stood. Below them stretched a murmurous complex of computers, men at desks and plotting consoles, messengers going soft-footed in and out. Nobody, from himself on down, bothered with spit-and-polish today. They had too much work on hand, coordinating the battle against Pickens' fleet. It had learned where they were from the ducal guards they chased off and had sought them out. Simply understanding that interaction of ships and energies was beyond mortal capacity.

He hated to tie up *Persei* when every gun spelled life to his outnumbered forces. She was half of the Nova-class dreadnaughts he had. But nothing less would hold the necessary equipment.

"We could do some fighting in addition," he said. "I've operated thus in the past."

"But that was before you were the Emperor," Oliphant replied

McCormac halted and glowered at him. The stout man chewed his cigar and plodded on: "Sir, we've few enough active supporters as is. Most bein's are just prayin' they won't get involved on either side. Why should anybody put everything at stake for the revolution, if he doesn't hope you'll bring him a better day? We could risk our control center, no doubt. But we can't risk you. Without you, the revolution 'ud fall apart 'fore Terran reinforcements could get here to suppress it."

McCormac clenched his fists and looked back at Satan. "Sorry," he mumbled. "I'm being childish."

" 'Tis forgivable," Oliphant said. "Two of your boys in combat—"

"And how many other people's boys? Human or xeno, they die, they're maimed. . . . Well." McCormac leaned over the balcony rail and studied the big display tank on the deck beneath him. Its colored lights gave only a hint of the information—itself partial and often unreliable—that flowed through the computers. But such three-dimensional pictures occasionally stimulated the spark of genius which no known civilization has succeeded in evoking from an electronic brain.

According to the pattern, his tactics were proving out. He had postulated that destruction of the factories on Satan would be too great an economic disaster for cautious Dave Pickens to hazard. Therefore the Josipists would be strictly enjoined not to come near the planet. Therefore McCormac's forces would have a privileged sanctuary. That would make actions possible to them which otherwise were madness. Of course, Pickens might charge straight in anyway; that contingency must be provided against. But if so, McCormac need have no compunctions about using Satan for shield and backstop. Whether it was destroyed or only held by his fleet, its products were denied the enemy. In time, that was sure to bring disaffection and weakness.

But it looked as if Pickens was playing safe—and getting mauled in consequence.

"S'pose we win," Oliphant said. "What next?"

It had been discussed for hours on end, but McCormac seized the chance to think past this battle. "Depends on what power the opposition has left. We want to take over as large a volume of space as possible without overextending ourselves. Supply and logistics are worse problems for us than

89

combat, actually. We aren't yet organized to replace losses or even normal consumption."

"Should we attack Ifri?"

"No. Too formidable. If we can cut it off, the same purpose is better served. Besides, eventually we'll need it ourselves."

"Llynathawr, though? I mean . . . well, we do have information that your lady was removed by some government agent—" Oliphant stopped, seeing what his well-meant speech had done.

McCormac stood alone, as if naked on Satan, for a while. Finally he could say: "No. They're bound to defend it with everything they have. Catawrayannis would be wiped out. Never mind Kathryn. There're too many other Kathryns around."

Can an Emperor afford such thoughts?

A visiscreen chimed and lit. A jubilant countenance looked forth. "Sir—Your Majesty—we've won!"

"What?" McCormac needed a second to understand.

"Positive, Your Majesty. Reports are pouring in, all at once. Still being evaluated, but, well, we haven't any doubt. It's almost like reading their codes."

A piece of McCormac's splintering consciousness visualized that possibility. The reference was not to sophont-sophont but machine-machine communication. A code was more than changed; the key computers were instructed to devise a whole new language, which others were then instructed to learn and use. Because random factors determined basic elements of the language, decipherment was, if not totally impossible, too laborious a process to overtake any prudent frequency of innovation. Hence the talk across space between robots, which wove their ships into a fleet, was a virtually unbreakable riddle to foes, a nearly infallible recognition signal to friends. The chance of interpreting it had justified numerous attempts throughout history at boarding or hijacking a vessel, however rarely they succeeded and however promptly their success caused codes to be revised. If you could learn a language the hostile machines were still using—

No. A daydream. McCormac forced his attention back to the screen. "Loss of *Zeta Orionis* probably decided him. They're disengaging everywhere." *I must get busy. We should harry them while they retreat, though not too far. Tactical improvisations needed.* "Uh, we've confirmed that *Vixen* is untouched. *John's ship.* "No report from *New Phobos*, but no positive reason to fear for her." *Colin's ship. Bob's with me.* "A moment, please. Important datum. . . . Sir, it's conirmed, *Aquilae* suffered heavy damage. She's almost certainly their flagship, you know. They won't be meshing any too well. We can eat them one at a time!" *Dave, are you alive?*

"Very good, Captain," McCormac said. "I'll join you right away on the command deck."

Aaron Snelund let the admiral stand, miserable in blue and gold, while he chose a cigaret from a jeweled case, rolled it in his fingers, sniffed the fragrance of genuine Terra-grown Crown grade marijuana, inhaled it into lighting, sat most gracefully down on his chair of state, and drank the smoke. No one else was in the room, save his motionless Gorzunians. The dynasculps were turned off. The animation was not, but its music was, so that masked lords and ladies danced without sound through a ballroom 200 light-years and half a century distant.

"Superb," Snelund murmured when he had finished. He nodded at the big gray-haired man who waited. "At ease."

Pickens did not relax noticeably. "Sir—" His voice was higher than before. Overnight he had become old.

Snelund interrupted him with a wave. "Don't trouble, Admiral. I have studied the reports. I know the situation consequent on your defeat. One is not necessarily illiterate, even with respect to the Navy's abominable prose, just because one is a governor. Is one?"

"No, Your Excellency."

Snelund lounged back, cross-legged, eyelids drooping. "I did not call you here for a repetition *viva voce* of what I have read," he continued mildly. "No, I wished for a chat that would be candid because private. Tell me, Admiral, what is your advice to me?"

"That's . . . in my personal report . . . sir."

Snelund arched his brows.

Sweat trickled down Pickens' cheeks. "Well, sir," he groped, "our total remaining power must be not greatly inferior to the, the enemy's. If we count what did not go to Satan. We can consolidate a small volume of space, hold it, let him have the rest. The Merseian confrontation can't go on forever. When we have heavy reinforcements, we can go out for a showdown battle."

"Your last showdown was rather disappointing, Admiral."

A tic vibrated one corner of Pickens' mouth. "The governor has my resignation."

"And has not accepted it. Nor will."

"Sir!" Pickens' mouth fell open.

"Be calm." Snelund shifted his tone from delicate sarcasm

to kindliness, his manner from idle humor to vigilance. "You didn't disgrace yourself, Admiral. You just had the misfortune to clash with a better man. Were you less able, little would have been salvaged from your defeat. As matters went, you rescued half your force. You lack imagination, but you have competence: a jewel of high price in these degenerate times. No, I don't want your resignation. I want you to continue in charge."

Pickens trembled. Tears stood in his eyes. "Sit down," Snelund invited. Pickens caved into a chair. Snelund kindled another cigaret, tobacco, and let him recover some equilibrium before saying:

"Competence, professionalism, sound organization and direction—you can supply those. I will supply the imagination. In other words, from here on I dictate policies for you to execute. Is that clear?"

His question lashed. Pickens gulped and croaked, "Yes, sir." It had been a precision job for Snelund, these past days, making the officer malleable without destroying his usefulness —an exacting but enjoyable task.

"Good. Good. Oh, by the way, smoke if you wish," the governor said. "Let me make clear what I plan.

"Originally I counted on applying various pressures through Lady McCormac. Then that dolt Flandry disappeared with her." A rage that boiled like liquid helium: "Have you any inkling what became of them?"

"No, sir," Pickens said. "Our Intelligence section hasn't yet succeeded in infiltrating the enemy. That takes time. . . . Er, from what we can piece together, she doesn't seem to have rejoined her husband. But we've had no word about her arrival anywhere else, like maybe on Terra."

"Well," Snelund said, "I don't envy Citizen Flandry once I get back." He rolled smoke around in his lungs until coolness returned. "No matter, really. The picture has changed. I've been rethinking this whole affair.

"What you propose, letting McCormac take most of the sector without resistance while we wait for help, is apparently the conservative course. Therefore it's in fact the most deadly dangerous. He must be counting on precisely that. Let him be proclaimed Emperor on scores of worlds, let him marshal their resources and arrange their defenses with that damnable skill he owns—and quite probably, when the Terran task force comes, it won't be able to dislodge him. Consider his short interior lines of communication. Consider popular enthusiasm roused by his demagogues and xenagogues. Consider the likelihood of more and more defections to his side

92

as long as his affairs run smoothly. Consider the virus spreading beyond this sector, out through the Empire, until it may indeed happen that one day he rides in triumph through Archopolis!"

Pickens stuttered, "I, I, I had thought of those things, Your Excellency."

Snelund laughed. "Furthermore, assuming the Imperium can put him down, what do you expect will become of you and, somewhat more significantly from this point of view, me? It will not earn us any medals that we allowed an insurrection and then could not quench it ourselves. Tongues will click. Heads will wag. Rivals will seize the opportunity to discredit. Whereas, if we can break Hugh McCormac unaided in space, clearing the way for my militia to clean out treason on the planets—well, kudos is the universal currency. It can buy us a great deal if we spend it wisely. Knighthood and promotion for you; return in glory to His Majesty's court for me. Am I right?"

Pickens moistened his lips. "Individuals like us shouldn't count. Not when millions and millions of lives—"

"But they belong to individuals too, correct? And if we serve ourselves, we serve the Imperium simultaneously, which we swore to do. Let us have no bleeding-heart unrealism. Let us get on with our business, the scotching of this rebellion."

"What does the governor propose?"

Snelund shook a finger. "Not propose, Admiral. Decree. We will thresh out details later. But in general, your mission will be to keep the war fires burning. True, our critical systems must be heavily guarded. But that will leave you with considerable forces free to act. Avoid another large battle. Instead raid, harass, hit and run, never attack a rebel group unless it's unmistakably weaker, make a special point of preying on commerce and industry."

"Sir? Those are our people!"

"McCormac claims they're his. And, from what I know of him, the fact that he'll be the cause of their suffering distress at our hands will plague him, will hopefully make him less efficient. Mind you, I don't speak of indiscriminate destruction. On the contrary, we shall have to have justifiable reasons for hitting every civilian target we do. Leave these decisions to me. The idea is, essentially, to undermine the rebel strength."

Snelund sat erect. One fist clenched on a chair arm. His hair blazed like a conqueror's brand. "Supply and replacement," he said ringingly. "Those are going to be McCormac's nemesis. He may be able to whip us in a stand-up battle. But

93

he can't whip attrition. Food, clothing, medical supplies, weapons, tools, spare parts, whole new ships, a navy must have them in steady flow or it's doomed. Your task will be to plug their sources and choke their channels."

"Can that be done, sir, well enough and fast enough?" Pickens asked. "He'll fix defenses, arrange convoys, make counterattacks."

"Yes, yes, I know. Yours is a single part of the effort, albeit a valuable one. The rest is to deny McCormac an effective civil service."

"I don't, uh, don't understand, sir."

"Not many do," Snelund said. "But think what an army of bureaucrats and functionaries compose the foundation of any government. It's no difference whether they are paid by the state or by some nominally private organization. They still do the day-to-day work. They operate the spaceports and traffic lanes, they deliver the mail, they keep the electronic communication channels unsnarled, they collect and supply essential data, they oversee public health, they hold crime in check, they arbitrate disputes, they allocate scarce resources. . . . Need I go on?"

He smiled wider. "Confidentially," he said, "the lesson was taught me by experience out here. As you know, I had various changes in policy and administrative procedure that I wished to put into effect. I was only successful to a degree, chiefly on backward planets with no real indigenous civil services. Otherwise, the bureaucrats dragged their feet too much. It's not like the Navy, Admiral. I would press an intercom button, issue a top priority order—and nothing would happen. Memos took weeks or months to go from desk to desk. Technical objections were argued comma by comma. Interminable requests for clarification made their slow ways back to me. Reports were filed and forgotten. It was like dueling a fog. And I couldn't dismiss the lot of them. Quite apart from legalities, I had to have them. There were no replacements for them.

"I intend to give Hugh McCormac a taste of that medicine."

Pickens shifted uneasily. "How, sir?"

"That's a matter I want to discuss this afternoon. We must get word to those planets. The little functionaries must be persuaded that it isn't in their own best interest to serve the rebellion with any zeal. Their natural timidity and stodginess work in our favor. If, in addition, we bribe some, threaten others, perhaps carry out an occasional assassination or bombing—Do you follow? We must plant our agents throughout McCormac's potential kingdom before he can take possession of it and post his guards. Then we must keep up the pressure—agents smuggled in, for example; propaganda; disruption of interstellar transportation by your raiders—Yes, I do believe we can bring McCormac's civil service machinery to a crawling, creaking slowdown. And without it, his navy starves. Are you with me, Admiral?"

Pickens swallowed. "Yes, sir. Of course."

"Good." Snelund rose. "Come along to the conference room. My staff's waiting. We'll thresh out specific plans. Would you like a stimpill? The session will probably continue till all hours."

They had learned of him, first on Venus, then on Terra, then in Sector Alpha Crucis: voluptuary he was, but when he saw a chance or a threat that concerned himself, twenty demons could not outwork him.

XI

Kathryn estimated the distance from Thunderstone to Port Frederiksen as about 2000 kilometers. But that was map distance, the kind that an aircar traversed in a couple of hours, a spacecraft in minutes or seconds. Aground and afoot, it would take weeks.

Not only was the terrain difficult, most of it was unknown to the Didonians. Like the majority of primitives, they seldom ventured far beyond their home territory. Articles of trade normally went from communion to communion rather than cross-country in a single caravan. Hence the three who accompanied the humans must feel their own way. In the mountains especially, this was bound to be a slow process with many false choices.

Furthermore, the short rotation period made for inefficient

travel. The autochthons refused to move after dark, and Flandry was forced to agree it would be unwise in strange areas. The days were lengthening as the season advanced; at midsummer they would fill better than seven hours out of the eight and three-quarters. But the Didonians could not take advantage of more than four or five hours. The reason was, again, practical. En route, away from the richer diet provided by their farms, a noga must eat—for three—whatever it could find. Vegetable food is less caloric than meat. The natives had to allow ample time for fueling their bodies.

"Twenty-four of us humans," Flandry counted. "And the sixteen we're leaving behind, plus the good doctor, also have appetites. I don't know if our rations will stretch."

"We can supplement some with native food," Kathryn reassured him. "There're levo compounds in certain plants and animals, same as terrestroid biochemistries involve occasional dextros. I can show you and the boys what they look like."

"Well, I suppose we may as well scratch around for them, since we'll be oysting so much in camp."

"Oystin'?"

"What oysters do. Mainly sit." Flandry ruffled his mustache. "Damn, but this is turning into a loathsome fungus! The two items I did not think to rescue would have to be scissors and a mirror."

Kathryn laughed. "Why didn't you speak before? They have scissors here. Clumsy, none too sharp, but you can cut hair with them. Let me be your barber."

Her hands across his head made him dizzy. He was glad that she let the men take care of themselves.

They were all quite under her spell. He didn't think it was merely because she was the sole woman around. They vied to do her favors and show her courtesies. He wished they would stop, but couldn't well order it. Relationships were strained already.

He was no longer the captain to them, but the commander: his brevet rank, as opposed to his lost status of shipmaster. They cooperated efficiently, but it was inevitable that discipline relaxed, even between enlisted men and other officers. He felt he must preserve its basic forms around himself. This led to a degree of—not hostility, but cool, correct aloofness as regarded him, in distinction to the camaraderie that developed among the rest.

One night, happening to wake without showing it, he overheard a muted conversation among several. Two were declaring their intention not just to accept internment, but to join

96

McCormac's side if its chances looked reasonable when they got to the base. They were trying to convince their friends to do likewise. The friends declined, for the time being at any rate, but good-naturedly. That was what disturbed Flandry: that no one else was disturbed. He began regular eavesdropping. He didn't mean to report anyone, but he did want to know where every man stood. Not that he felt any great need for moralistic justification. The snooping was fun.

That started well after the party had left Thunderstone. The three Didonians were named by Kathryn as Cave Discoverer, Harvest Fetcher, and, to human amusement, Smith. It was more than dubious if the entities thought of themselves by name. The terms were convenient designations, based on personal qualities or events of past life. The unit animals had nothing but individual signals.

Often they swapped around, to form such combinations as Iron Miner, Guardian Of North Gate, or Lightning Struck The House. Kathryn explained that this, was partly for a change, partly to keep fresh the habits and memories which constituted each entity, and partly a quasi-religious rite.

"Oneness is the ideal in this culture, I'm learnin', as 'tis in a lot of others," she told Flandry. "They consider the whole world to be potenti'ly a single entity. By ceremonies, mystic contemplation, hallucinogenic foods, or whatever, they try to merge with it. An everyday method is to make frequent new interconnections. The matin' season, 'round the autumnal equinox, is their high point of the year, mainly 'cause of the ecstatic, transcendental 'speriences that then become possible."

"Yes, I imagine a race like this has some interesting sexual variations," Flandry said. She flushed and looked away. He didn't know why she should react so, who had observed life as a scientist. Associations with her captivity? He thought not. She was too vital to let that cripple her long; the scars would always remain, but by now she had her merriment back. Why, then, this shyness with him?

They were following a ridge. The country belonged to another communion which, being akin to Thunderstone, had freely allowed transit. Already they had climbed above the jungle zone. Here the air was tropical by Terran standards, but wonderfully less wet, with a breeze to lave the skin and caress the hair and carry scents not unlike ginger. The ground was decked with spongy brown carpet weed, iridescent blossoms, occasional stands of arrowbrush, grenade, and lantern tree. A mass of land coral rose to the left, its red and blue the more vivid against the sky's eternal silver-gray.

None of the Didonians were complete. One maintained heesh's noga-ruka linkage, the other two rukas were off gathering berries, the three krippos were aloft as scouts. Separated, the animals could carry out routine tasks and recognize a need for reunion when it arose.

Besides their own ruka-wielded equipment—including spears, bows, and battleaxes—the nogas easily carried the stuff from the spaceboat. Thus liberated, the men could outpace the ambling quadrupeds. With no danger and no way to get lost hereabouts, Flandry had told them to expedite matters by helping the rukas. They were scattered across the hill.

Leaving him alone with Kathryn.

He was acutely conscious of her: curve of breast and hip beneath her coverall, free-swinging stride, locks blowing free and bright next to the sun-darkened skin, strong face, great green-gold eyes, scent of warm flesh. . . . He changed the subject at once. "Isn't the, well, pantheistic concept natural to Didonians?"

"No more than monotheism's natural, inevitable, in man," Kathryn said with equal haste. "It depends on culture. Some exalt the communion itself, as an entity distinct from the rest of the world, includin' other communions. Their rites remind me of human mobs cheerin' an almighty State and its director. They tend to be warlike and predatory." She pointed ahead, where mountain peaks were vaguely visible. "I'm 'fraid we've got to get past a society of that kind. 'Tis one reason why they weren't keen on this trip in Thunderstone. Word travels, whether or not entities do. I had to remind Many Thoughts 'bout our guns."

"People who don't fear death make wicked opponents," Flandry said. "However, I wouldn't suppose a Didonian exactly enjoys losing a unit; and heesh must have the usual desire to avoid pain."

Kathryn smiled, at ease once more. "You learn fast. Ought to be a xenologist yourself."

He shrugged. "My business has put me in contact with various breeds. I remain convinced we humans are the weirdest of the lot; but your Didonians come close. Have you any idea how they evolved?"

"Yes, some paleontology's been done. Nowhere near enough. Why is it we can always find money for a war and're always pinched for everything else? Does the first cause the second?"

"I doubt that. I think people naturally prefer war."

"Someday they'll learn."

"You have insufficient faith in man's magnificent ability to

98

ignore what history keeps yelling at him," Flandry said. Immediately, lest her thoughts turn to Hugh McCormac who wanted to reform the Empire: "But fossils are a less depressing subject. What about evolution on Dido?"

"Well, near's can be told, a prolonged hot spell occurred —like millions of years long. The ancestors of the nogas fed on soft plants which drought made scarce. 'Tis thought they took to hangin' 'round what trees were left, to catch leaves that ancestral rukas tore loose in the course of gatherin' fruit. Belike they had a tickbird relationship with the proto-krippos. But trees were dyin' off too. The krippos could spy forage a far ways off and guide the nogas there. Taggin' 'long, the rukas got protection to boot, and repaid by strippin' the trees.

"At last some of the animals drifted to the far eastern end of the Barcan continent. 'Twas afflicted, as 'tis yet, with a nasty kind of giant bug that not only sucks blood, but injects a microbe whose action keeps the wound open for days or weeks. The ancestral nogas were smaller and thinner-skinned than today's. They suffered. Prob'ly rukas and krippos helped them, swattin' and eatin' the heaviest swarms. But then they must've started sippin' the blood themselves, to supplement their meager diet."

"I can take it from there," Flandry said. "Including hormone exchange, mutually beneficial and cementing the alliance. It's lucky that no single-organism species happened to develop intelligence. It'd have mopped the deck with those awkward early three-ways. But the symbiosis appears to be in business now. Fascinating possibilities for civilization."

"We haven't exposed them to a lot of ours," Kathryn said. "Not just 'cause we want to study them as they are. We don't know what might be good for them, and what catastrophic."

"I'm afraid that's learned by trial and error," Flandry answered. "I'd be intrigued to see the result of raising some entities from birth"—the krippos were viviparous too—"in Technic society."

"Why not raise some humans 'mong Didonians?" she flared.

"I'm sorry." *You make indignation beautiful.* "I was only snakkering. Wouldn't do it in practice, not for anything. I've seen too many pathetic cases. I did forget they're your close friends."

Inspiration! "I'd like to become friends with them myself," Flandry said. "We have a two or three months' trip and buckets of idle time in camp ahead of us. Why don't you teach me the language?"

She regarded him with surprise. "You're serious, Dominic?"

"Indeed. I don't promise to retain the knowledge all my life. My head's overly cluttered with cobwebby information as is. But for the present, yes, I do want to converse with them directly. It'd be insurance for us. And who knows, I might come up with a new scientific hypothesis about them, too skewball to have occurred to any Aenean."

She laid a hand on his shoulder. That was her way; she liked to touch people she cared about. "You're no Imperial, Dominic," she said. "You belong with us."

"Be that as it may—" he said, confused.

"Why do you stand with Josip? You know what he is. You've seen his cronies, like Snelund, who could end by replacin' him in all but name. Why don't you join us, your kind?"

He knew why not, starting with the fact that he didn't believe the revolution could succeed and going on to more fundamental issues. But he could not tell her that, on this suddenly magical day. "Maybe you'll convert me," he said. "Meanwhile, what about language lessons?"

"Why, 'course."

—Flandry could not forbid his men to sit in, and a number of them did. By straining his considerable talent, he soon disheartened them and they quit. After that, he had Kathryn's whole notice for many hours per week. He ignored the jealous stares, and no longer felt jealous himself when she fell into cheerful conversation with one of the troop or joined a campfire circle for singing.

Nor did it perturb him when Chief Petty Officer Robbins returned from an excursion with her in search of man-edible plants, wearing a black eye and a sheepish look. Unruffled, she came in later and treated Robbins exactly as before. Word must have spread, for there were no further incidents.

Flandry's progress in his lessons amazed her. Besides having suitable genes, he had been through the Intelligence Corps' unmercifully rigorous courses in linguistics and metalinguistics, semantics and metasemantics, every known trick of concentration and memorization; he had learned how to learn. Few civilian scientists received that good a training; they didn't need it as urgently as any field agent always did. Inside a week, he had apprehended the structures of Thunderstone's language and man's pidgin—no easy feat, when the Didonian mind was so absolutely alien.

Or was it? Given the basic grammar and vocabulary, Flandry supplemented Kathryn's instruction by talking, mainly with Cave Discoverer. It went ridiculously at first, but after weeks he got to the point of holding real conversations. The Didonian was as interested in him and Kathryn as she was in heesh. She took to joining their colloquies, which didn't bother him in the least.

Cave Discoverer was more adventurous than average. Heesh's personality seemed more clearly defined than the rest, including any others in the party which incorporated heesh's members. At home heesh hunted, logged, and went on rambling explorations when not too busy. Annually heesh traveled to the lake called Golden, where less advanced communions held a fair and Cave Discoverer traded metal implements for their furs and dried fruits. There heesh's noga had the custom of joining with a particular ruka from one place and krippo from another to make the entity Raft Farer. In Thunderstone, besides Many Thoughts, Cave Discoverer's noga and ruka belonged to Master Of Songs; heesh's krippo (female) to Leader Of Dance; heesh's ruka to Brewmaster; and all to various temporary groups.

Aside from educational duties, none of them linked indiscriminately. Why waste the time of a unit that could make part of an outstanding entity, in junction with units less gifted? The distinction was somewhat blurred but nonetheless real in Thunderstone, between "first families" and "proles." No snobbery or envy appeared to be involved. The attitude was pragmatic. Altruism within the communion was so taken for granted that the concept did not exist.

Or thus went Flandry's and Kathryn's impressions. She admitted they might be wrong. How do you probe the psyche of a creature with three brains, each of which remembers its share in other creatures and, indirectly, remembers things that occurred generations before it was born?

Separately, the nogas were placid, though Kathryn said they became furious if aroused. The krippos were excitable and musical; they produced lovely clear notes in intricate patterns. The rukas were restless, curious, and playful. But these were generalizations. Individual variety was as great as for all animals with well-developed nervous systems.

Cave Discoverer was in love with heesh's universe. Heesh looked forward with excitement to seeing Port Frederiksen and wondered about the chance of going somewhere in a spaceship. After heesh got straight the basic facts of astronomy, xenology, and galactic politics, heesh's questions sharpened until Flandry wondered if Didonians might not be inherently more intelligent than men. Could their technological backwardness be due to accidental circumstances that would no longer count when they saw the possibility of making systematic progress?

The future could be theirs, not ours, Flandry thought. *Kathryn would reply, "Why can't it be everybody's?"*

Meanwhile the expedition continued—through rain, gale, fog, heat, strange though not hostile communions, finally highlands where the men rejoiced in coolness. There, however, the Didonians shivered, and went hungry in a land of sparse growth, and, despite their krippos making aerial surveys, often blundered upon impassable stretches that forced them to retrace their steps and try again.

It was here, in High Maurusia, that battle smote them.

XII

The easiest way to reach one pass was through a canyon. During megayears, a river swollen by winter rains had carved it, then shrunken in summer. Its walls gave protection from winds and reflected some heat; this encouraged plant life to spring up every dry season along the streambed, where accumulated soil was kinder to feet than the naked rock elsewhere. Accordingly, however twisted and boulder-strewn, it appeared to offer the route of choice.

The scenery was impressive in a gaunt fashion. The river rolled on the party's left, broad, brown, noisy and dangerous despite being at its low point. A mat of annual plants made a border whose sober hues were relieved by white and scarlet blossoms. Here and there grew crooked trees, deep-rooted, adapted to inundation. Beyond, the canyon floor reached barren: tumbled dark rocks, fantastically eroded pinnacles and mesas, on to the talus slopes and palisades. Gray sky, diffuse and shadowless light, did not bring out color or detail very well; that was a bewildering view. But human lungs found the air mild, dry, exhilarating.

Two krippos wheeled on watch overhead. Harvest Fetcher stayed complete, and every ruka rode a noga. The outworlders walked behind, except for Kathryn, Flandry, and Havelock. She was off to the right, wrapped in her private thoughts. This landscape must have made her homesick for Aeneas. The commander and the ensign kept out of their companions' earshot.

"Damn it, sir, why do we take for granted we'll turn ourselves in at Port Frederiksen without a fight?" Havelock was protesting. "This notion our case is hopeless, it's encouraging treasonable thoughts."

Flandry refrained from saying he was aware of that. Havelock had been less standoffish than the rest; but a subtle barrier persisted, and Flandry had cultivated him for weeks before getting this much confidence. He knew Havelock had a girl on Terra.

"Well, Ensign," he said, "I can't make promises, for the reason that I'm not about to lead us to certain death. As you imply, though, the death may not necessarily be certain. Why don't you feel out the men? I don't want anyone denounced to me," *having a pretty fair idea myself,* "but you might quietly find who's . . . let's not say trustworthy, we'll assume everybody is, let's say enthusiastic. You might, still more quietly, alert them to stand by in case I do decide on making a break. We'll talk like this, you and I, off and on. More off than on, so as not to provoke suspicion. We'll get Kathryn to describe the port's layout, piecemeal, and that'll be an important element in what I elect to do."

You, Kathryn, will be more important.

"Very good, sir," Havelock said. "I hope——"

Assault burst forth.

The party had drawn even with a nearby rock mass whose bottom was screened by a row of crags. From behind these plunged a score of Didonians. Flandry had an instant to think, *Ye devils, they must've hid in a cave!* Then the air was full of arrows. "Deploy!" he yelled. "Fire! Kathryn, get down!"

A shaft went *whoot* by his ear. A noga bugled, a ruka screamed. Bellyflopping, Flandry glared over the sights of his blaster at the charging foe. They were barbarically decorated with pelts, feather blankets, necklaces of teeth, body paint. Their weapons were neolithic, flint axes, bone-tipped arrows and lances. But they were not less deadly for that, and the ambush had been arranged with skill.

He cast a look to right and left. Periodically while traveling, he had drilled his men in ground combat techniques.
Today it paid off. They had formed an arc on either side of
him. Each who carried a gun—there weren't many small
arms aboard a warship—was backed by two or three com-
rades with spears or daggers, ready at need to assist or to
take over the trigger.

Energy beams flared and crashed. Slugthrowers hissed,
stunners buzzed. A roar of voices and hoofs echoed above
the river's clangor. A krippo turned into flame and smoke, a
ruka toppled to earth, a noga ran off bellowing its anguish.
Peripherally, Flandry saw more savages hit.

But whether in contempt for death or sheer physical momentum, the charge continued. The distance to cover was
short; and Flandry had not imagined a noga could gallop that
fast. The survivors went by his line and fell on the Thunderstone trio before he comprehended it. One man barely rolled
clear of a huge gray-blue body. The airborne flyers barely
had time to reunite with their chief partners.

"Kathryn!" Flandry shouted into the din. He leaped erect
and whirled around. The melee surged between him and her.
For a second he saw how Didonians fought. Nogas, nearly
invulnerable to edged weapons, pushed at each other and
tried to gore. Rukas stabbed and hacked; krippos took what
shelter they could, while grimly maintaining linkage, and
buffeted with their wings. The objective was to put an oppo-
nent out of action by eliminating heesh's rider units.

Some mountaineer nogas, thus crippled by gunfire, blundered around in the offing. A few two-member entities held
themselves in reserve, for use when a ruka or krippo went
down in combat. Eight or nine complete groups surrounded
the triangular formation adopted by the three from Thunderstone.

No, two and a half. By now Flandry could tell them apart.
Harvest Fletcher's krippo must have been killed in the arrow
barrage. The body lay transfixed, pathetically small, tailfeath-
ers ruffled by a slight breeze, until a noga chanced to trample
it into a smear. Its partners continued fighting, automatically
and with lessened skill.

"Get those bastards!" somebody called. Men edged warily
toward the milling, grunting, yelling, hammering interlocked
mass. It was hard to understand why the savages were ignor-
ing the humans, who had inflicted all the damage on them.
Was the sight so strange as not to be readily comprehensible?

Flandry ran around the struggle to see what had become of
Kathryn. *I never gave her a gun!* he knew in agony.

Her tall form broke upon his vision. She had retreated a distance, to stand beneath a tree she could climb if attacked. His Merseian blade gleamed in her grasp, expertly held. Her mouth was drawn taut but her eyes were watchful and steady.

He choked with relief. Turning, he made his way to the contest.

A stone ax spattered the brains of Smith's ruka. Cave Discoverer's ruka avenged the death in two swift blows—but, surrounded, could not defend his back. A lance entered him. He fell onto the horn of a savage noga, which tossed him high and smashed him underfoot when he landed.

The humans opened fire.

It was butchery.

The mountaineer remnants stampeded down the canyon. Not an entity among them remained whole. A young Terran stood over a noga, which was half cooked but still alive, and gave it the *coup de grace;* then tears and vomit erupted from him. The Thunderstoners could assemble one full person at a time. Of the possible combinations, they chose Guardian Of North Gate, who went about methodically releasing the wounded from life.

The entire battle, from start to finish, had lasted under ten minutes.

Kathryn came running. She too wept. "So much death, so much hurt—can't we help them?" A ruka stirred. He didn't seem wounded; yes, he'd probably taken a stun beam, and the supersonic jolt had affected him as it did a man. Guardian Of North Gate approached. Kathryn crouched over the ruka. "No! I forbid you."

The Didonian did not understand her pidgin, for only heesh's noga had been in Cave Discoverer. But her attitude was unmistakable. After a moment, with an almost physical shrug, heesh had heesh's ruka tie up the animal.

Thereafter, with what assistance the humans could give, heesh proceeded to care for the surviving Thunderstone units. They submitted patiently. A krippo had a broken leg, others showed gashes and bruises, but apparently every member could travel after a rest.

No one spoke aloud a wish to move from the battleground. No one spoke at all. Silent, they fared another two or three kilometers before halting.

In the high latitudes of Dido, nights around midsummer were not only short, they were light. Flandry walked beneath a sky blue-black, faintly tinged with silver, faintly adance

with aurora where some of Virgil's ionizing radiation pene-
trated the upper clouds. There was just sufficient luminance
for him not to stumble. Further off, crags and cliffs made
blacknesses which faded unclearly into the dusk. Mounting a
bluff that overlooked his camp, he saw its fire as a red wavering spark, like a dying dwarf star. The sound of the river
belled subdued but clear through cool air. His boots
scrunched on gravel; occasionally they kicked a larger rock.
An unknown animal trilled somewhere close by.

Kathryn's form grew out of the shadows. He had seen her
depart in this direction after the meal she refused, and
guessed she was bound here. When he drew close, her face
was a pale blur.

"Oh . . . Dominic," she said. The outdoor years had
trained her to use more senses than vision.

"You shouldn't have gone off alone." He stopped in front
of her.

"I had to."

"At a minimum, carry a gun. You can handle one, I'm
sure."

"Yes. 'Course. But I won't, after today."

"You must have seen violent deaths before."

"A few times. None that I helped cause."

"The attack was unprovoked. To be frank, I don't regret
anything but our own losses, and we can't afford to lament
them long."

"We were crossin' the natives' country," she said. "Maybe
they resented that. Didonians have territorial instincts, same
as man. Or maybe our gear tempted them. No slaughter, no
wounds, if 'tweren't for our travelin'."

"You've lived with the consequences of war," his inner
pain said harshly. "And this particular fracas was an incident
in your precious revolution."

He heard breath rush between her lips. Remorse stabbed
him. "I, I'm sorry, Kathryn," he said. "Spoke out of turn.
I'll leave you alone. But please come back to camp."

"No." At first her voice was almost too faint to hear. "I
mean . . . let me stay out a while." She seized his hand. "But
of your courtesy, don't you skite either. I'm glad you came,
Dominic. You understand things."

Do I? Rainbows exploded within him.

They stood a minute, holding hands, before she laughed
uncertainly and said: "Again, Dominic. Be practical with
me."

You're brave enough to live with your sorrows, he thought,
but strong and wise enough to turn your back on them the

106

first chance that comes, and cope with our enemy the universe.

He wanted, he needed one of his few remaining cigarets; but he couldn't reach the case without disturbing her clasp, and she might let go. "Well," he said in his awkwardness, "I imagine we can push on, day after tomorrow. They put Lightning Struck The House together for me after you left." All heesh's units had at various times combined with those that had been in Cave Discoverer: among other reasons, for heesh to gain some command of pidgin.

"We discussed things. It'd take longer to return, now, than finish our journey, and the incompletes can handle routine. The boys have gotten good at trailsmanship themselves. We'll bear today's lesson in mind and avoid places where bushwhackers can't be spotted from above. So I feel we can make it all right."

"I doubt if we'll be bothered any more," Kathryn said with a return of energy in her tone. "News'll get 'round."

"About that ruka we took prisoner."

"Yes? Why not set the poor beast free?"

"Because . . . well, Lightning isn't glad we have the potential for just one full entity. There're jobs like getting heavy loads down steep mountainsides which're a deal easier and safer with at least two, especially seeing that rukas are their hands. Furthermore, most of the time we can only have a single krippo aloft. The other will have to stay in a three-way, guiding the incompletes and making decisions, while we're in this tricky mountainland. One set of airborne eyes is damn little."

"True." He thought he heard the rustle of her hair, which she had let grow longer, as she nodded. "I didn't think 'bout that 'fore, too shocked, but you're right." Her fingers tensed on his. "Dominic! You're not plannin' to use the prisoner?"

"Why not? Lightning seems to like the idea. Been done on occasion, heesh said."

"In emergencies. But . . . the conflict, the—the cruelty—"

"Listen, I've given these matters thought," he told her. "Check my facts and logic. We'll force the ruka into linkage with the noga and krippo that were Cave Discoverer's—the strongest, most sophisticated entity we had. He'll obey at gun point. Besides, he has to drink blood or he'll starve, right? A single armed man alongside will prevent possible contretemps. However, two units against one ought to prevail by themselves. We'll make the union permanent, or nearly so, for the duration of our trip. That way, the Thunderstone patterns should go fast and deep into the ruka. I daresay the

107

new personality will be confused and hostile at first; but heesh ought to cooperate with us, however grudgingly."

"Well—"

"We need heesh, Kathryn! I don't propose slavery. The ruka won't be absorbed. He'll give—and get—will learn something to take home to his communion—maybe an actual message of friendship, an offer to establish regular relations —and gifts, when we release him here on our way back to Thunderstone."

She was silent, until: "Audacious but decent, yes, that's you. You're more a knight than anybody who puts 'Sir' in front of his name, Dominic."

"Oh, Kathryn!"

And he found he had embraced her and was kissing her, and she was kissing him, and the night was fireworks and trumpets and carousels and sacredness.

"I love you, Kathryn, my God, I love you."

She broke free of him and moved back. "No. . . ." When he groped toward her, she fended him off. "No, please, please, don't. Please stop. I don't know what possessed me. . . ."

"But I love you," he cried.

"Dominic, no, we've been too long on this crazy trek. I care for you more'n I knew. But I'm Hugh's woman."

He dropped his arms and stood where he was, letting the spirit bleed out of him. "Kathryn," he said, "for you I'd join your side."

"For my sake?" She came close again, close enough to lay hands on his shoulders. Half sobbing, half laughing: "You can't dream how glad I am."

He stood in the fragrance of her, fists knotted, and replied, "Not for your sake. For you."

"What?" she whispered, and let him go.

"You called me a knight. Wrong. I won't play wistful friend-of-the-family rejected suitor. Not my style. I want to be your man myself, in every way that a man is able."

The wind lulled, the river boomed.

"All right," Flandry said to the shadow of her. "Till we reach Port Frederiksen. No longer. He needn't know. I'll serve his cause and live on the memory."

She sat down and wept. When he tried to comfort her, she thrust him away, not hard but not as a coy gesture either. He moved off a few meters and chainsmoked three cigarets.

Finally she said, "I understand what you're thinkin' Dominic. If Snelund, why not you? But don't you see th difference? Startin' with the fact I do like you so much?"

108

He said through the tension in his throat, "I see you're loyal to an arbitrary ideal that originated under conditions that don't hold good any more."

She started to cry afresh, but it sounded dry, as if she had spent her tears.

"Forgive me," Flandry said. "I never meant to hurt you. Would've cut my larynx out first. We won't speak about this, unless you want to. If you change your mind, tomorrow or a hundred years from tomorrow, while I'm alive I'll be waiting."

Which is perfectly true, gibed a shard of him, *though I am not unaware of its being a well-composed line, and nourish a faint hope that my noble attitude will yet draw her away from that bucketheaded mass murderer Hugh McCormac.*

He drew his blaster and pushed it into her cold unsteady clasp. "If you must stay here," he said, "keep this. Give it back to me when you come down to camp. Goodnight."

He turned and left. There went through him: *Very well, if I have no reason to forswear His Majesty Josip III, let me carry on with the plan I'm developing for the discomfiture of his unruly subjects.*

XIII

The group spent most of the next day and night sleeping. Then Flandry declared it was needful to push harder forward than hitherto. The remaining Didonian(s?) formed several successive entities, as was the custom when important decisions were to be reached, and agreed. For them, these uplands were bleak and poor in forage. Worse lay ahead, especially in view of the hurts and losses they had suffered. Best get fast over the mountains and down to the coastal plain.

That was a Herculean undertaking. The humans spent

most of their time gathering food along the way for the nogas. When exhaustion forced a stop, it likewise forced sleep. Kathryn was athletic, but she remained a woman of thirty, trying to match the pace and toil of men in their teens and twenties. She had small chance to talk, with Flandry or anyone, on trail or off.

He alone managed that. His company looked mutinous when he announced that he must be exempted from most of the labor in order to establish communication with the new entity. Havelock jollied them out of their mood.

"Look, you've seen the Old Man in action. You may not like him, but he's no shirker and no fool. Somebody has to get that xeno cooperating. If nothing else, think how we need a guide through this damned arse-over-tip country. . . . Why not Kathryn? Well, she *is* the wife of the man who got us dumped where we are. It wouldn't improve our records, that we trusted her with something this critical. . . . Sure, you'd better think about your records, those of you who plan on returning home."

Flandry had given him a confidential briefing.

At the outset, talk between man and Didonian was impossible. The personality fought itself, captive ruka pouring hate and fear of the whole troop into a noga and krippo which detested his communion. And the languages, habits, attitudes, thought patterns, the whole *Weltanschauungen* were at odds, scarcely comprehensible mutually. Linked under duress, the entity slogged along, sometimes sullen, sometimes dazed, always apt to lash out on a half insane impulse. Twice Flandry had to scramble; the noga's horn missed him by centimeters.

He persevered. So did the two animals which had been in Cave Discoverer. And the noga had had experience with alien partners, the two which had annually joined him to make Raft Farer. Flandry tried to imagine what the present situation felt like, and couldn't. Schizophrenia? A racking conflict of opposed desires, akin to his own as regarded Kathryn McCormac versus the Terran Empire? He doubted it. The being he confronted was too foreign.

He sought to guide its coalescence, initially by his behavior, later by his words. Once the ruka nervous system was freed from expecting imminent torture or death, meshing was natural. Language followed. Part of the Thunderstone vocabulary had died with Cave Discoverer's ruka. But some was retained, and more was acquired when, for a time, the krippo was replaced by the other ruka. The savage unit objected violently—it turned out that his culture regarded a two-species three-way as perverted—but got no choice in the matter. The

110

hookup of neurones as well as blood vessels was automatic when tendrils joined. Flandry exerted his linguistic skills to lead the combinations through speech exercises. Given scientific direction, the inborn Didonian adaptability showed quick results.

By the time the party had struggled across the passes and were on the western slope of the mountains, Flandry could talk to the mind he had called into being.

The entity did not seem especially fond of heeshself. The designation heesh adopted, more by repeated usage than by deliberate selection, was a grunt which Kathryn said might translate as "Woe." She had little to do with heesh, as much because the obvious emotional trouble distressed her as because of weariness. That suited Flandry. Conversing with Woe, alone except for a sentry who did not understand what they uttered, he could build on the partial amnesia and the stifled anger, to make what he would of the Didonian.

"You must serve me," he said and repeated. "We may have fighting to do, and you are needed in place of heesh who is no more. Trust and obey none save me. I alone can release you in the end—with rich reward for both your communions. And I have enemies among my very followers."

He would have told as elaborate, even as truthful a story as required. But he soon found it was neither necessary nor desirable. Woe was considerably less intelligent as well as less knowledgeable than Cave Discoverer. To heesh, the humans were supernatural figures. Flandry, who was clearly their chieftain and who furthermore had been midwife and teacher to heesh's consciousness, was a vortex of *mana*. Distorted recollections of what he and Kathryn had related to Cave Discoverer reinforced what he now said about conflict among the Powers. The ruka brain, most highly developed of the three, contributed its mental set to the personality of Woe, whose resulting suspicion of heesh's fellow units in the group was carefully *not* allayed by Flandry.

When they had reached the foothills, Woe was his tool. Under the influence of noga and krippo, the Didonian had actually begun looking forward to adventuring in his service.

How he would use that tool, if at all, he could not predict. It would depend on the situation at journey's terminus.

Kathryn took him aside one evening. Steamy heat and jungle abatis enclosed them. But the topography was easier and the ribs of the Didonians were disappearing behind regained flesh. He and she stood in a canebrake, screened from the world, and regarded each other.

"Why haven't we talked alone, Dominic?" she asked him.

111

Her gaze was grave, and she had taken both his hands in hers.

He shrugged. "Too busy."

"More'n that. We didn't dare. Whenever I see you, I think of— You're the last person after Hugh that I'd want to hurt."

"After Hugh."

"You're givin' him back to me. No god could do anything more splendid."

"I take it, then," he said jaggedly, "that you haven't reconsidered about us."

"No. You make me wish I could wish to. But—Oh, I'm so grieved. I hope so hard you'll sqon find your right woman."

"I've done that," he said. She winced. He realized he was crushing her hands, and eased the pressure. "Kathryn, my darling, we're in the homestretch, but my offer stays the same. Us—from here to Port Frederiksen—and I'll join the revolution."

"That's not worthy of you," she said, whitening.

"I know it isn't," he snarled. "Absolute treason. For you, I'd sell my soul. You have it anyway."

"How can you say treason?" she exclaimed as if he had struck her.

"Easy. Treason, treason, treason. You hear? The revolt's worse than evil, it's stupid. You—"

She tore loose and fled. He stood alone till night entirely surrounded him. *Nu, Flandry,* he thought once, *what ever made you suppose the cosmos was designed for your personal convenience?*

Thereafter Kathryn did not precisely avoid him. That would have been impossible under present circumstances. Nor was it her desire. On the contrary, she often smiled at him, with a shyness that seared, and her tone was warm when they had occasion to speak. He answered somewhat in kind. Yet they no longer left the sight of their companions.

The men were wholly content with that. They swarmed about her at every chance, and this flat lowland gave them plenty of chances. No doubt she sincerely regretted injuring Flandry; but she could not help it that joy rose in her with every westward kilometer and poured from her as laughter and graciousness and eager response. Havelock had no problem in getting her to tell him, in complete innocence, everything she knew about the Aenean base.

"Damn, I hate to use her like that!" he said, reporting to his commander in privacy.

"You're doing it for her long-range good," Flandry replied.

"An excuse for a lot of cruelty and treachery in the past."

"And in the future. Yeh. However . . . Tom, we're merely collecting information. Whether we do anything more turns entirely on how things look when we arrive. I've told you before, I won't attempt valorous impossibilities. We may very well go meekly into internment."

"If we don't, though—"

"Then we'll be helping strike down a piece of foredoomed foolishness a little quicker, thereby saving quite a few lives. We can see to it that those lives include Kathryn's." Flandry clapped the ensign's back. "Slack off, son. Figure of speech, that; I'd have had to be more precocious than I was to mean it literally. Nevertheless, slack off, son. Remember the girl who's waiting for you."

Havelock grinned and walked away with his shoulders squared. Flandry stayed behind a while. *No particular girl for me, ever,* he reflected, *unless Hugh McCormac has the kindness to get himself killed. Maybe then—*

Could I arrange that somehow—if she'd never know I had —could I? A daydream, of course. But supposing the opportunity came my way . . . could I?

I honestly can't say.

Like the American Pacific coast (on Terra, Mother Terra), the western end of Barca wrinkled in hills which fell abruptly down to the sea. When she glimpsed the sheen of great waters, Kathryn scrambled up the tallest tree she could find. Her shout descended leaf by leaf, as sunshine does: "Byrsa Head! Can't be anything else! We're less'n 50 kilometers south of Port Frederiksen!"

She came down in glory. And Dominic Flandry was unable to say more than: "I'll proceed from here by myself."

"What?"

"A flit, in one of the spacesuits. First we'll make camp in some pleasant identifiable spot. Then I'll inquire if they can spare us an aircraft. Quicker than walking."

"Let me go 'long," she requested, ashiver with impatience.

You can go 'long till the last stars burn out, if you choose. Only you don't choose. "Sorry, no. Don't try to radio, either. Listen, but don't transmit. How can we tell what the situation is? Maybe bad; for instance, barbarians might have taken advantage of our family squabble and be in occupation. I'll check. If I'm not back in . . . oh . . . two of these small inexpensive days"— *You always have to clown, don't you?*— "Lieutenant Valencia will assume command and use his own judgment." *I'd prefer Havelock. Valencia's too sympathetic to the revolt. Still, I have to maintain the senior officer convention if I'm to lie to you, my dearest, if I'm to have any chance of harming your cause, my love until I die.*

His reminder dampened hilarity. The troop settled in by a creek, under screening trees, without fire. Flandry suited up. He didn't give any special alert to Woe or to his several solid allies among the men. They had arranged a system of signals many marches before.

"Be careful, Dominic," Kathryn said. Her concern was a knife in him. "Don't risk yourself. For all our sakes."

"I won't," he promised. "I enjoy living." *Oh, yes, I expect to keep on enjoying it, whether or not you will give it any real point.* "Cheers." He activated the impeller. In a second or two, he could no longer see her waving goodbye.

He flew slowly, helmet open, savoring the wind and salt smells as he followed the coastline north. The ocean of moonless Dido had no real surf, it stretched gray under the gray sky, but in any large body of water there is always motion and mystery; he saw intricate patterns of waves and foam, immense patches of weed and shoals of swimming animals, a rainstorm walking on the horizon. To his right the land lifted from wide beaches, itself a quilt of woods and meadows, crossed by great herds of grazers and flocks of flyers. *By and large*, he thought, *planets do well if man lets them be.*

Despite everything, his pulse accelerated when Port Frederiksen appeared. Here was his destiny.

The base occupied a small, readily defensible peninsula. It was sufficiently old to have become a genuine community. The prefab sheds, shelters, and laboratories were weathered, vine-begrown, almost a part of the landscape; and among them stood houses built from native wood and stone, in a breeze-inviting style evolved for this place, and gardens and a park. Kathryn had said the population was normally a thousand but doubtless far less during the present emergency. Flandry saw few people about.

His attention focused on the spacefield. If it held a mere interplanetary vessel, his optimum bet was to surrender. But no. Hugh McCormac had left this prized outpost a hyperdrive warship. She wasn't big—a Conqueror-class subdestroyer, her principal armament a blaster cannon, her principal armor speed and maneuverability, her normal complement twenty-five—but she stood rakish on guard, and Flandry's heart jumped.

That's my baby! He passed close. She didn't appear to have more than the regulation minimum of two on duty, to

114

judge from the surrounding desertion. And why should she? Given her controls, instruments, and computers, a single man could take her anywhere. Port Frederiksen would know of approaching danger in time for her personnel to go aboard. Otherwise they doubtless helped the civilians.

Emblazoned above her serial number was the name *Erwin Rommel*. Who the deuce had that been? Some Germanian? No, more likely a Terran, resurrected from the historical files by a data finder programmed to christen several score thousand of Conquerors.

People emerged from buildings. Flandry had been noticed. He landed in the park. "Hello," he said. "I've had a bit of a shipwreck."

During the next hour, he inquired about Port Frederiksen. In return, he was reasonably truthful. He told of a chance encounter with an enemy vessel, a crash landing, a cross-country hike. The main detail he omitted was that he had not been on McCormac's side.

If his scheme didn't work, the Aeneans would be irritated when they learned the whole truth; but they didn't strike him as the kind who would punish a ruse of war.

Essentially they were caretakers: besides the *Rommel*'s crew, a few scientists and service personnel. Their job was to maintain the fruitful relationship with neighboring Didonians and the fabric of the base. Being what they were, they attempted in addition to continue making studies.

Physically, they were isolated. Interplanetary radio silence persisted, for Josipist ships had raided the Virgilian System more than once. Every month or so, a boat from Aeneas brought supplies, mail, and news. The last arrival had been only a few days before. Thus Flandry got an up-to-date account of events.

From the Aenean viewpoint, they were dismal. Manufacture, logistics, and communications were falling apart beneath Hugh McCormac. He had given up trying to govern any substantial volume of space. Instead, he had assigned forces to defend individually the worlds which had declared for him. They were minimal, those forces. They hampered but could not prevent badgering attacks by Snelund's squadrons. Any proper flotilla could annihilate them in detail.

Against that development, McCormac kept the bulk of his fleet around Satan. If the Josipists gathered in full strength, he would learn of it from his scouts, go meet the armada, and rely on his tactical abilities to scatter it.

"But they know that," Director Jowett said. He stroked his white beard with a hand that trembled. "They won't give our

115

Emperor the decisive battle he needs. I wonder if Snelund 'ull even call for reinforcements when Terra can spare them. He may simply wear us down. I'm sure he'd enjoy our havin' a long agony."

"Do you think we should yield?" Flandry asked.

The old head lifted. "Not while our Emperor lives!"

Folk being starved for visitors, Flandry had no trouble in learning more than he needed to know. They fell in readily with a suggestion he made. Rather than dispatch aircars to fetch his companions, why not use the *Rommel?* No instrumental readings or flashed communication from Aeneas indicated any immediate reason to hold her in condition red. Jowett and her captain agreed. Of course, there wouldn't be room for the whole gang unless most of the crew stayed behind. The few who did ride along could use the practice.

Flandry had sketched alternative plans. However, this simplified his task.

He guided the ship aloft and southward. En route, he called the camp. Somebody was sure to be listening on a helmet radio. "All's fine," he said. "We'll land on the beach exactly west of your location and wait for you. Let me speak with Ensign Havelock. . . . Tom? It's Q. Better have Yuan and Christopher lead off."

That meant that they were to don their armor.

The ship set down. Those who manned her stepped trustfully out onto the sand. When they saw the travelers emerge from the woods, they shouted their welcomes across the wind.

Two gleaming metal shapes hurtled into view above the treetops. A second afterward, they were at hover above the ship, with blasters aimed.

"Hands up, if you please," Flandry said.

"What?" the captain yelled. A man snatched at his sidearm. A beam sizzled from overhead, barely missing him. Sparks showered and steam puffed where it struck.

"Hands up, I repeat," Flandry snapped. "You'd be dead before any shot of yours could penetrate."

Sick-featured, they obeyed. "You're being hijacked," he told them. "You might as well start home at once. It'll take you some hours on shank's mare."

"You Judas." The captain spat.

Flandry wiped his face and answered, "Matter of definition, that. Get moving." Yuan accompanied the group for some distance.

Beforehand, suddenly drawn guns had made prisoners of men whose loyalty was in question. More puzzled than angry,

116

Lightning Struck The House guided the uncoupled units aboard. Woe marched Kathryn up the ramp. When he saw her, Flandry found business to do on the other side of the ship.

With his crew embarked and stations assigned, he hauled gravs. Hovering above the settlement, he disabled the interplanetary transmitter with a shot to its mast. Next he broadcast a warning and allowed the people time to evacuate. Finally he demolished other selected installations.

The Aeneans would have food, shelter, medicine, ground defenses. But they wouldn't be going anywhere or talking to anybody until a boat arrived from Aeneas, and none was due for a month.

"Take her east, Citizen Havelock," Flandry directed. "We'll fetch our chums at Thunderstone and let off the surplus livestock. And, yes, we'll lay in some food for the new Didonian. I think I may have use for heesh."

"Where at, sir?"

"Llynathawr. We'll leave this system cautiously, not to be spotted. When well into space, we'll run at maximum hyperspeed to Llynathawr."

"Sir?" Havelock's mien changed from adoration to puzzlement. "I beg the captain's pardon, but I don't understand. I mean, you've turned a catastrophe into a triumph, we've got the enemy's current code and he doesn't know we do, but shouldn't we make for Ifri? Especially when Kathryn—"

"I have my reasons, " Flandry said. "Never fear, she will not go back to Snelund." His own expression was so forbidding that no one dared inquire further.

XIV

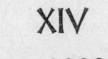

Again the metal narrowness, chemical-tainted air, incessant beat of driving energies, but also the wintry wonder of stars, the steady brightening of a particular golden point among them. From Virgil to Llynathawr, in this ship, the flit was less than two standard days.

Flandry held captain's mast. The wardroom was too cramped for everybody, but audiovisual intercoms were tuned. The crew saw him seated, in whites that did not fit well but were nonetheless the full uniform of his rank. Like theirs, his body was gaunt, the bones standing sharply forth in his countenance, the eyes unnaturally luminous by contrast with a skin burned almost black. Unlike most of them, he showed no pleasure in his victory.

"Listen carefully," he said. "In an irregular situation such as ours, it is necessary to go through various formalities." He took the depositions which, entered in the log, would retroactively legalize his seizure of *Rommel* and his status as her master.

"Some among you were put under arrest," he went on. "That was a precautionary measure. In a civil war, one dares not trust a man without positive confirmation, and obviously I couldn't plan a surprise move with our entire group. The arrest is hereby terminated and the subjects ordered released. I will specifically record and report that their detention was in no way meant to reflect on their loyalty or competence, and that I recommend every man aboard for promotion and a medal."

He did not smile when they cheered. His hard monotone went on: "By virtue of the authority vested in me, and in conformance with Naval regulations on extraordinary recruitment, I am swearing the sophont from the planet Dido, known to us by the name Woe, into His Majesty's armed service on a temporary basis with the rating of common spaceman. In view of the special character of this being, the enrollment shall be entered as that of three new crewpeople."

Laughter replied. They thought his imp had spoken. They were wrong.

"All detection systems will be kept wide open," he continued after the brief ceremony. "Instantly upon contact with any Imperial ship, the communications officer will signal surrender and ask for an escort. I daresay we'll all be arrested when they board us, till our bona fides can be established. However, I trust that by the time we assume Llynathawr orbit, we'll be cleared.

"A final item. We have an important prisoner aboard. I told Ensign Havelock, who must have told the rest of you, that Lady McCormac will not be returned to the custody of Sector Governor Snelund. Now I want to put the reason on

118

official though secret record, since otherwise our action would be grounds for court-martial.

"It is not in the province of Naval officers to make political decisions. Because of the circumstances about Lady McCormac, including the questionable legality of her original detention, my judgment is that handing her over to His Excellency would *be* a political decision, fraught with possibly ominous consequences. My duty is to deliver her to Naval authorities who can dispose of her case as they find appropriate. At the same time, we cannot in law refuse a demand for her person by His Excellency.

"Therefore, as master of this vessel, and as an officer of the Imperial Naval Intelligence Corps, charged with an informational mission and hence possessed of discretionary powers with respect to confidentiality of data, et cetera, I classify Lady McCormac's presence among us as a state secret. She will be concealed before we are boarded. No one will mention that she has been along, then or at any future date, until such time as the fact may be granted public release by a qualified governmental agency. To do so will constitute a violation of the laws and rules on security, and subject you to criminal penalties. If asked, you may say that she escaped just before we left Dido. Is that understood?"

Reverberating shouts answered him.

He sat back. "Very well," he said tiredly. "Resume your stations. Have Lady McCormac brought here for interview."

He switched off the com. His men departed. *I've got them in my pocket,* he thought. *They'd ship out for hell if I were the skipper.* He felt no exaltation. *I don't really want another command.*

He opened a fresh pack of the cigarets he had found among stocked rations. The room enclosed him in drabness. Under the machine noises and the footfalls outside, silence grew.

But his heart knocked when Kathryn entered. He rose.

She shut the door and stood tall in front of it. Her eyes, alone in the spacecraft, looked on him in scorn. His knife had stayed on her hip.

When she didn't speak and didn't speak, he faltered, "I—I hope the captain's cabin—isn't too uncomfortable."

"How do you aim to hide me?" she asked. The voice had its wonted huskiness, and nothing else.

"Mitsui and Petrović will take the works out of a message capsule. We can pad the casing and tap airholes that won't be noticed. You can have food and drink and, uh, what els

119

you'll need. It'll get boring, lying there in the dark, but shouldn't be longer than twenty or thirty hours."

"Then what?"

"If everything goes as I expect, we'll be ordered into parking orbit around Llynathawr," he said. "The code teams won't take much time getting their readouts from our computers. Meanwhile we'll be interrogated and the men assigned temporarily to Catawrayannis Base till extended leave can be given them. Procedure cut and dried and quick; the Navy's interested in what we bring, not our adventures while we obtained it. Those can wait for the board of inquiry on *Asieneuve's* loss. The immediate thing will be to hit the rebels before they change their code.

"I'll assert myself as captain of the *Rommel*, on detached service. My status could be disputed; but in the scramble to organize that attack, I doubt if any bureaucrat will check the exact wording of regs. They'll be happy to let me have the responsibility for this boat, the more so when my roving commission implies that I need the means to rove.

"As master, I'm required to keep at least two hands on watch. In parking orbit, that's a technicality, no more. And I've seen to it that technically, Woe is three crewmen. I'm reasonably confident I can fast-talk my way out of any objections to heesh. It's such a minor-looking matter, a method of not tying up two skilled spacers who could be useful elsewhere.

"When you're alone, heesh will let you out."

Flandry ran down. He had lectured her in the same way as he might have battered his fists on a steel wall.

"Why?" she said.

"Why what?" He stubbed out his cigaret and reached for another.

"I can understand . . . maybe . . . why you did what you've done . . . to Hugh. I wouldn't've thought it of you, I saw you as brave and good enough to stand for what's right, but I can imagine that down underneath, your spirit is small.

"But what I can't understand, can't grasp," Kathryn sighed, "is that you—after everything—are bringin' me back to enslavement. If you hadn't told Woe to seize me, there's not a man of your men who wouldn't've turned away while I ran into the forest."

He could not watch her any longer. "You're needed," he mumbled.

"For what? To be wrung dry of what little I know? To be dangled 'fore Hugh in the hope 'twill madden him? To be made an example of? And it doesn't matter whether 'tis an

120

example of Imperial justice or Imperial mercy, whatever was me will die when they kill Hugh." She was not crying, not reproaching. Peripherally, he saw her shake her head in a slow, bewildered fashion. "I *can't* understand."

"I don't believe I'd better tell you yet," he pleaded. "Too many variables in the equation. Too much improvising to do. But—"

She interrupted. "I'll play your game, since 'tis the one way I can at least 'scape from Snelund. But I'd rather not be with you." Her tone continued quiet. " 'Twould be a favor if you weren't by when they put me in that coffin."

He nodded. She left. Woe's heavy tread boomed behind her.

Whatever his shortcomings, the governor of Sector Alpha Crucis set a magnificent table. Furthermore, he was a charming host, with a rare gift for listening as well as making shrewd and witty comments. Though most of Flandry crouched like a panther behind his smile, a part reveled in this first truly civilized meal in months.

He finished his narrative of events on Dido as noiseless live servants cleared away the last golden dishes, set forth brandy and cigars, and disappeared. "Tremendous!" applauded Snelund. "Utterly fascinating, that race. Did you say you brought one back? I'd like to meet the being."

"That's easily arranged, Your Excellency," Flandry said. "More easily than you perhaps suspect."

Snelund's brows moved very slightly upward, his fingers tensed the tiniest bit on the stem of his snifter. Flandry relaxed, inhaled the bouquet of his own drink, twirled it to enjoy the play of color within the liquid, and sipped in conscious counterpoint to the background lilt of music.

They sat on an upper floor of the palace. The chamber was not large, but graciously proportioned and subtly tinted. A wall had been opened to the summer evening. Air wandered in from the gardens bearing scents of rose, jasmine, and less familiar blossoms. Downhill glistered the city, lights in constellations and fountains, upward radiance of towers, firefly dance of aircars. Traffic sounds were a barely perceptible murmur. You had trouble believing that all around and spilling to the stars, it roared with preparations for war.

Nor was Snelund laying on any pressure. Flandry might have removed Kathryn McCormac hence for "special interrogation deemed essential to the maximization of success probability on a surveillance mission" in sheer impudence. He might have lost first his ship and last his prisoner in sheer

121

carelessness. But after he came back with a booty that should allow Admiral Pickens to give the rebellion a single spectacular deathblow, without help from Terra and with no subsequent tedious inspection of militia operations, the governor could not well be aught but courteous to the man who saved his political bacon.

Nevertheless, when Flandry requested a secret talk, it had not been with the expectation of dinner *tête-à-tête*.

"Indeed?" Snelund breathed.

Flandry glanced across the table at him: wavy, fiery hair, muliebrile countenance, gorgeous purple and gold robe, twinkle and shimmer of jewelry. Behind that, Flandry thought, were a bowel and a skull.

"The thing is, sir," he said, "I had a delicate decision to make."

Snelund nodded, smiling but with a gaze gone flat and hard as two stones. "I suspected that, Commander. Certain aspects of your report and behavior, certain orders you issued with a normally needless haste and authoritative ring, were not lost on me. You have me to thank for passing the word that I felt you should not be argued with. I was, ah, curious as to what you meant."

"I do thank Your Excellency." Flandry started his cigar. "This matter's critical to you too, sir. Let me remind you of my dilemma on Dido. Lady McCormac became extremely popular with my men."

"Doubtless." Snelund laughed. "I taught her some unusual tricks."

I have no weapons under this blue and white dress uniform, Aaron Snelund. I have nothing but my hands and feet. And a black belt in karate, plus training in other techniques. Except for unfinished business, I'd merrily let myself be executed, in fair trade for the joy of dismantling you.

Because the creature must recall what her soul had been like when he flayed it open, and might be probing veracity now, Flandry gave him a sour grin. "No such luck, sir. She even refused *my* proposition, which fact I pray you to declare a top secret. But—well, there she was, the only woman, handsome, able, bright. Toward the end, most were a touch in love with her. She'd spread the impression that her stay here had been unpleasant. To be frank, sir, I feared a mutiny if the men expected she'd be remanded to you. Bringing in the code was too crucial to risk."

"So you connived at her escape." Snelund sipped. "That's tacitly realized by everyone, Commander. A sound judgment,

122

whether or not we dare put it in the record. She can be tracked down later."

"But sir, I didn't."

"What!" Snelund sat bolt erect.

Flandry said fast: "Let's drop the euphemisms, sir. She made some extremely serious accusations against you. Some people might use them to buttress a claim that your actions were what caused this rebellion. I didn't want that. If you've read much history, you'll agree nothing works like a Boadicea—no?—a martyr, especially an attractive female martyr, to create trouble. The Empire would suffer. I felt it was my duty to keep her. To get the men's agreement, I had to convince them she would not be returned here. She'd go to a Naval section, where rules protect prisoners and testimony isn't likely to be suppressed."

Snelund had turned deadpan. "Continue," he said.

Flandry sketched his means of smuggling her in. "The fleet should be assembled and ready to depart for Satan in about three days," he finished, "now that scouts have verified the enemy is still using the code I brought. I'm not expected to accompany it. I am expected, though, by my men, to obtain orders for myself that will send the *Rommel* to Ifri, Terra, or some other place where she'll be safe. They'll have ways of finding out whether I do. You know how word circulates in any set of offices. If I don't—I'm not sure that secrecy will bind every one of those lads. And disclosure would inconvenience you, sir, at this highly critical time."

Snelund drained his brandy glass and refilled it. The little *glug-glug* sounded loud across the music. "Why do you tell me?"

"Because of what I've said. As a patriot, I can't allow anything that might prolong the rebellion."

Snelund studied him. "And she refused you?" he said at length.

Spite etched Flandry's tones. "I don't appreciate that, from third-hand goods like her." With quick smoothness: "But this is beside the point. My obligation . . . to you, Your Excellency, as well as to the Imperium—"

"Ah, yes." Snelund eased. "It does no harm to have a man in your debt who is on his way up, does it?"

Flandry looked smug.

"Yes-s-s, I think we resonate, you and I," Snelund said. "What is your suggestion?"

"Well," Flandry replied, "as far as officialdom knows, *Rommel* contains no life other than my multiple Didonian.

123

And heesh will never talk. If my orders were cut tonight—not specifically to anywhere, let's say, only for 'reconnaissance and report at discretion, employing minimal crew'—a phone call by Your Excellency to someone on Admiral Pickens' staff would take care of that—I could go aboard and depart. My men would relax about Lady McCormac. When they haven't heard news of her in a year or two—well, reassignment will have scattered them and feelings will have cooled. Oblivion is a most valuable servant, Your Excellency."

"Like yourself," Snelund beamed. "I do believe our careers are going to be linked, Commander. If I can trust you—"

"Come see for yourself," Flandry proposed.

"Eh?"

"You said you'd be interested in meeting my Didonian anyway. It can be discreet. I'll give you the *Rommel*'s orbital elements and you go up alone in your flitter, not telling anybody where you're bound." Flandry blew a smoke ring. "You might like to take personal charge of the execution. To make sure it's done in a manner suitable to the crime. We could have hours."

Then he waited.

Until sweat made beads on Snelund's skin and an avid voice said, "Yes!"

Flandry hadn't dared hope to catch the prize for which he angled. Had he failed, he would have made it his mission in life to accomplish the same result by other methods. The fact left him feeling so weak and lightheaded that he wondered vaguely if he could walk out of there.

He did, after a period of conference and arrangement-making. A gubernatorial car delivered him at Catawrayannis Base, where he changed into working garb, accepted his orders, and got a flitter to the *Rommel*.

Time must be allowed for that craft to descend again, lest the pilot notice another and ornate one lay alongside. Flandry sat on the bridge, alone with his thoughts. The viewscreen showed him planet and stars, a huge calm beauty.

Vibration sounded in the metal, as airlocks joined and magnetronic grapples made fast. Flandry went down to admit his guest.

Snelund came through the airlock breathing hard. He carried a surgical kit. "Where is she?" he demanded.

"This way, sir." Flandry let him go ahead. He did not appear to have noticed Flandry's gun, packed in case of bodyguards. There weren't any. They might have gossiped.

Woe stood outside the captain's cabin. Xenological interest

124

or no, Snelund barely glanced at heesh and jittered while Flandry said in pidgin: "Whatever you hear, stay where you are until I command you otherwise."

The noga's horn dipped in acknowledgment. The ruka touched the ax at his side. The krippo sat like a bird of prey.

Flandry opened the door. "I brought you a visitor, Kathryn," he said.

She uttered a noise that would long run through his nightmares. His Merseian war knife flew into her hand.

He wrenched the bag from Snelund and pinioned the man in a grip that was not to be shaken. Kicking the door shut behind him, he said, "Any way you choose, Kathryn. Any way at all."

Snelund began screaming.

XV

Seated at the pilot board of the gig, Flandry pushed controls to slide aside the housing and activate the viewscreens. Space leaped at him. The gloom of Satan and the glitter of stars drifted slowly past as *Rommel* swung around the planet and tumbled along her invariable plane. Twice he identified slivers of blackness crossing the constellations and the Milky Way: nearby warcraft. But unaided senses could not really prove to him that he was at the heart of the rebel fleet.

Instruments had done that as he drove inward, and several curt conversations once he came in range. Even when Kathryn spoke directly with Hugh McCormac, reserve stood between them. Warned by his communications officer what to expect, the admiral had had time to don a mask. How could he know it wasn't a trick? If he spoke to his wife at all, and not to an electronic shadow show, she might be under brainscrub, speaking the words that her operator projected into

125

her middle ear. Her own mostly impersonal sentences, uttered from a visage nearly blank, yet the whole of her unsteady, might lend credence to that fear. Flandry had been astonished. He had taken for granted she would cry forth in joy.

Was it perhaps a simple but strong wish for privacy, or was it that at this ultimate moment and ultimate stress she must fight too hard to keep from flying apart? There had been no chance to ask her. She obeyed Flandry's directive, revealing no secret of his, insisting that the two men hold a closed-door parley before anything else was done; and McCormac agreed, his voice rough and not altogether firm; and then things went too fast—the giving of directions, the study of meters, the maneuvers of approach and orbit matching—for Flandry to learn what she felt.

But while he prepared to go, she came from the cabin to which she had retreated. She seized his hands and looked into his eyes and whispered, "Dominic, I'm prayin' for both of you." Her lips brushed across his. They were cold, like her fingers, and tasted of salt. Before he could respond, she walked quickly away again.

Theirs had been a curious intimacy while they traveled hither. The red gift he had given her; the plan he laid out, and that she helped him perfect after she saw he was not to be moved from it; between times, dreamy talk of old days and far places, much reminiscence about little events on Dido —Flandry wondered if man and woman could grow closer in a wedded lifetime. In one aspect, yes, obviously they could; but that one they both shied off from speaking of.

And here came *Persei* into view and with her, one way or another, an end to everything which had been. The flagship loomed like a moon, mottled with thermostatic paint patterns, hilled with boat nacelles and gun turrets, thrusting out cannon and sensors like crystal forests. Satellite craft glinted around her. Indicator lights glowed on Flandry's board and his receiver said, "We have a lock on you. Go ahead."

He started the gravs. The gig left *Rommel* and surrendered to control from *Persei*. It was a short trip, but tense on both sides of the gap. How could McCormac be positive this was not a way to get a nuclear weapon inside his command vessel and detonate it? *He can't,* Flandry thought. *Especially when I wouldn't allow anyone to come fetch me. Of course that might well have been for fear of being captured by a boarding party, which indeed was partly the case, but just the same— He's courageous, McCormac. I detest him to his inmost cell, but he's courageous.*

126

A portal gaped and swallowed him. He sat for a minute hearing air gush back into the housing. Its personnel valves opened. He left the gig and went to meet the half dozen men who waited. They watched him somberly, neither hailing nor saluting.

He returned the stares. The insurrectionists were as marked by hunger and strain as he, but theirs was a less healthy, a sallowing, faintly grubby condition. "Relax," he said. "Inspect my vessel if you wish. No boobytraps, I assure you. Let's not dawdle, though."

"This way . . . please." The lieutenant who led the squad started off with rapid, stiff strides. Part of the group stayed behind, to check the boat. Those who walked at Flandry's back were armed. It didn't bother him. He had worse dangers to overcome before he could sleep.

They went through metal tunnels and caverns, past hundreds of eyes, in silence hardly broken save for the ship's pulse and breath. At the end, four marines guarded a door. The lieutenant addressed them and passed through. Saluting in the entrance, he said, "Commander Flandry, sir."

"Send him in," replied a deep toneless voice. "Leave us alone but stay on call."

"Aye, sir." The lieutenant stood aside. Flandry went by. The door closed with a soft hiss that betokened soundproofing.

Quiet lay heavy in the admiral's suite. This main room was puritanically furnished: chairs, a table, a couch, a plain rug, the bulkheads and overhead an undraped light gray. A few pictures and animations gave it some personality: family portraits, views from home, scenes of wilderness. So did a chess set and a bookshelf which held both codices and spools, both classics and scientific works. One of the inner doors was ajar, showing an office where McCormac must often toil after his watches. No doubt the bedroom was downright monastic, Flandry thought, the galley and bar seldom used, the—

"Greeting," McCormac said. He stood large, straight, gaunt as his men but immaculate, the nebula and stars frosty on his shoulders. He had aged, Flandry saw: more gray in the dark hair than pictures recorded, still less flesh in the bony countenance and more wrinkles, the eyes sunken while the nose and chin had become promontories.

"Good day." Flandry felt a moment's awe and inadequacy wash over him. He dismissed it with a measure of cold enjoyment.

"You might have saluted, Commander," McCormac said quietly.

"Against regulations," Flandry replied. "You've forfeited your commission."

"Have I? Well—" McCormac gestured. "Shall we sit down? Would you care for refreshment?"

"No, thanks," Flandry said. "We haven't time to go through the diplomatic niceties. Pickens' fleet will be on you in less than 70 hours."

McCormac lowered himself. "I am aware of that, Commander. We keep our scouts busy, you know. The mustering of that much strength could not be concealed. We're prepared for a showdown; we welcome it." He glanced up at the younger man and added: "You observe that I give you your proper rank. I am the Emperor of all Terran subjects. After the war, I plan on amnesty for nearly everyone who misguidedly opposed me. Even you, perhaps."

Flandry sat down too, opposite him, crossed ankle over knee, and grinned. "Confident, aren't you?"

"It's a measure of your side's desperation that it sent you in advance to try negotiating, with what you claim is my wife for a hostage." McCormac's mouth tightened. Momentarily, the wrath in him struck forth, though he spoke no louder. "I despise any man who'd lend himself to such a thing. Did you imagine I'd abandon everyone else who's trusted me to save any individual, however dear? Go tell Snelund and his criminals, there will be no peace or pardon for them, though they run to the ends of the universe; but there are ways and ways to die, and if they harm my Kathryn further, men will remember their fate for a million years."

"I can't very well convey that message," Flandry replied, "seeing that Snelund's dead." McCormac half rose. "What Kathryn and I came to let you know is that if you accept battle, you and your followers will be equally dead."

McCormac leaned over and seized Flandry by the upper arms, bruisingly hard. "What is this?" he yelled.

Flandry snapped that grip with a judo break. "Don't paw me, McCormac," he said.

They got back on their feet, two big men, and stood toe to toe. McCormac's fists were doubled. The breath whistled in and out of him. Flandry kept hands open, knees tense and a trifle bent, ready to move out of the way and chop downward. The impasse lasted thirty mortal seconds.

McCormac mastered himself, turned, stalked a few paces

off, and faced around again. "All right," he said as if being strangled. "I let you in so I could listen to you. Carry on."

"That's better." Flandry resumed his chair and took out a cigaret. Inwardly he shook and felt now frozen, now on fire. "The thing is," he said, "Pickens has your code."

McCormac rocked where he stood.

"Given that," Flandry said redundantly, "if you fight, he'll take you apart; if you retreat, he'll chivvy you to pieces; if you disperse, he'll snatch you and your bases in detail before you can rally. You haven't time to recode and you'll never be allowed the chance. Your cause is done, McCormac."

He waved the cigaret. "Kathryn will confirm it," he added. "She witnessed the whole show. Alone with her, you'll soon be able to satisfy yourself that she's telling the truth, under no chemical compulsions. You won't need any psych tests for that, I hope. Not if you two are the loving couple she claims.

"Besides, after talking to her, you're welcome to send a team over who'll remove my central computer. They'll find your code in its tapes. That'll disable my hyperdrive, of course, but I don't mind waiting for Pickens."

McCormac stared at the deck. "Why didn't she come aboard with you?" he asked.

"She's my insurance," Flandry said "She won't be harmed unless your side does something ridiculous like shooting at my vessel. But if I don't leave this one freely, my crew will take the appropriate measures."

Which I trust, dear Hugh, you will interpret as meaning that I have trained spacehands along, who'll speed away if you demonstrate bad faith. It's the natural assumption, which I've been careful to do nothing to prevent you from making. The datum that my crew is Woe, who couldn't navigate a flatboat across a swimming pool, and that heesh's orders are to do nothing no matter what happens . . . you're better off not receiving that datum right at once. Among other things, first I want to tell you some home truths.

McCormac lifted his head and peered closely. With the shock ridden out, his spirit and intelligence were reviving fast. "*Your* hostage?" he said from the bottom of his throat.

Flandry nodded while kindling his cigaret. The smoke soothed him the least bit. "Uh-huh. A long story. Kathryn will tell you most of it. But the upshot is, though I serve the Imperium, I'm here in an irregular capacity and without its knowledge."

"Why?"

Flandry spoke with the same chill steadiness as he regarded the other: "For a number of reasons, including that I'm Kathryn's friend. I'm the one who got her away from Snelund. I took her with me when I went to see what the chance was of talking you out of your lunacy. You'd left the Virgilian System, but one of your lovely barbarian auxiliaries attacked and wrecked us. We made it down to Dido and marched overland to Port Frederiksen. There I seized the warship from which the code was gotten, the same I now command. When I brought it to Llynathawr, my men and I kept Kathryn's presence secret. They think the cosmos of her too, you see. I lured Governor Snelund on board, and held him over a drain while she cut his throat. I'd have done worse, so'd you, but she has more decency in a single DNA strand than you or I will ever have in our whole organisms. She helped me get rid of the evidence because I want to return home. We tossed it on a meteorite trajectory into the atmosphere of an outer planet. Then we headed for Satan."

McCormac shuddered. "Do you mean she's gone over to your side—to you? Did you two—"

Flandry's cigaret dropped from lips yanked into a gorgon's lines. He surged up and across the deck, laid hold of McCormac's tunic, batted defending hands aside with the edge of his other palm and numbing force, shook the admiral and grated:

"Curb your tongue! You sanctimonious son of a bitch! If I had my wish, your pig-bled body would've been the one to burn through that sky. But there's Kathryn. There's the people who've followed you. There's the Empire. Down on your knees, McCormac, and thank whatever smug God you've taken on as your junior partner, that I have to find some way of saving your life because otherwise the harm you've done would be ten times what it is!"

He hurled the man from him. McCormac staggered against a bulkhead, which thudded. Half stunned, he looked upon the rage which stood before him, and his answering anger faded.

After a while, Flandry turned away. "I'm sorry," he said in a dull voice. "Not apologetic, understand. Only sorry I lost my temper. Unprofessional of me, especially when our time is scant."

McCormac shook himself. "I said I'd listen. Shall we sit down and begin over?" Flandry had to admire him a trifle for that.

They descended stiffly to the edges of their chairs. Flandry got out a new cigaret. "Nothing untoward ever happened between Kathryn and me," he said, keeping his eyes on the tiny cylinder. "I won't deny I'd have liked for it to, but it didn't. Her entire loyalty was, is, and forever will be to you. I think I've persuaded her that your present course is mistaken, but not altogether. And in no case does she want to go anyplace but where you go, help in anything but what you do. Isn't that an awesome lot to try to deserve?"

McCormac swallowed. After a moment: "You're a remarkable fellow, Commander. How old are you?"

"Half your age. And yet I have to tell you the facts of life."

"Why should I heed you," McCormac asked, but subduedly, "when you serve that abominable government? When you claim to have ruined my cause?"

"It was ruined anyway. I know how well your opposition's Fabian strategy was working. What we hope to do—Kathryn and I—we 'hope to prevent you from dragging more lives, more treasure, more Imperial strength down with you."

"Our prospects weren't that bad. I was evolving a plan—"

"The worst outcome would have been your victory."

"What? Flandry, I . . . I'm human, I'm fallible, but *anyone* would be better on the throne than that Josip who appointed that Snelund."

With the specter of a smile, because his own fury was dying out and a measure of pity was filling the vacuum, Flandry replied: "Kathryn still accords with you there. She still feels you're the best imaginable man for the job. I can't persuade her otherwise, and haven't tried very hard. You see, it doesn't matter whether she's right or wrong. The point is, you might have given us the most brilliant administration in history, and nevertheless your accession would have been catastrophic."

"Why?"

"You'd have destroyed the principle of legitimacy. The Empire will outlive Josip. Its powerful vested interests, its cautious bureaucrats, its size and inertia, will keep him from doing enormous harm. But if you took the throne by force, why shouldn't another discontented admiral do the same in another generation? And another and another, till civil wars rip the Empire to shreds. Till the Merseians come in, and the barbarians. You yourself hired barbarians to fight Terrans, McCormac. No odds whether or not you took precautions, the truth remains that you brought them in, and sooner or later we'll get a rebel who doesn't mind conceding them territory. And the Long Night falls."

131

"I could not disagree more," the admiral retorted with vehemence. "Restructuring a decadent polity—"

Flandry cut him off. "I'm not trying to convert you either. I'm simply explaining why I did what I did." *We need not tell you that I'd have abandoned my duty for Kathryn. That makes no difference any more*—interior laughter jangled—*except that it would blunt the edge of my sermon.* "You can't restructure something that's been irreparably undermined. All your revolution has managed to do is get sophonts killed, badly needed ships wrecked, trouble brewed that'll be years in settling—on this critical frontier."

"What should I have done instead?" McCormac disputed. "Leave my wife and myself out of it. Think only what Snelund had already done to this sector. What he would do if and when he won back to Terra. Was there another solution but to strike at the root of our griefs and dangers?"

" 'Root'—*radix*—you radicals are all alike," Flandry said. "You think everything springs from one or two unique causes, and if only you can get at them, everything will automatically become paradisical. History doesn't go that way. Read some and see what the result of every resort to violence by reformists has been."

"Your theory!" McCormac said, flushing. "I . . . we were faced with a fact."

Flandry shrugged. "Many moves were possible," he said. "A number had been started: complaints to Terra, pressure to get Snelund removed from office or at least contained in his scope. Failing that, you might have considered assassinating him. I don't deny he was a threat to the Empire. Suppose, specifically, after your friends liberated you, you'd gotten together a small though efficient force and mounted a raid on the palace for the limited purposes of freeing Kathryn and killing Snelund. Wouldn't that have served?"

"But what could we have done afterward?"

"You'd have put yourselves outside the law." Flandry nodded. "Same as I've done, though I hope to hide the guilt I don't feel. Quite aside from my personal well-being, the fact would set a bad precedent if it became public. Among your ignorances, McCormac, is that you don't appreciate how essential a social lubricant hypocrisy is."

"We couldn't have . . . skulked."

"No, you'd have had to do immediately what you and many others now have to do regardless—get out of the Empire."

"Are you crazy? Where to?"

Flandry rose once more and looked down upon him.

"You're the crazy man," he said. "I suppose we are decadent these days, in that we never seem to think of emigration. Better stay home, we feel, and cling to what we have, what we know, our comforts, our assurances, our associations . . . rather than vanish forever into that big strange universe . . . even when everything we cling to is breaking apart in our hands. But the pioneers worked otherwise. There's room yet, a whole galaxy beyond these few stars we think we control, out on the far end of one spiral arm.

"You can escape if you start within the next several hours. With that much lead, and dispersal in addition, your ships ought to be able to pick up families, and leave off the men who don't want to go. Those'll have to take their chances with the government, though I imagine necessity will force it to be lenient. Set a rendezvous at some extremely distant star. None of your craft will likely be pursued much past the border if they happen to be detected.

"Go a long way, McCormac, as far as you possibly can. Find a new planet. Found a new society. Never come back."

The admiral raised himself too. "I can't abandon my responsibilities," he groaned.

"You did that when you rebelled," Flandry said. "Your duty is to save what you can, and live the rest of your life knowing what you wrought here. Maybe the act of leading people to a fresh beginning, maybe that'll console you." *I'm sure it will in time. You have a royal share of self-righteousness.* "And Kathryn. She wants to go. She wants it very badly." He caught McCormac's gaze. "If ever a human being had a right to be taken from this civilization, she does."

McCormac blinked hard.

"Never come back," Flandry repeated. "Don't think of recruiting a barbarian host and returning. You'd be the enemy then, the real enemy. I want your word of honor on that. If you don't give it to me, and to Kathryn, she won't be allowed to rejoin you, whatever you may do to me. *I lie like a wet rag.*" If you do give it, and break it, she will not pardon you.

"In spite of your behavior, you are an able leader. You're the one man who can hope to carry the emigration off, in as short a while as you have to inform, persuade, organize, act. Give me your word, and Kathryn will ride back in my gig to you."

McCormac covered his face. "Too sudden. I can't—"

"Well, let's thresh out a few practical questions first, if you like. I've pondered various details beforehand."

"But—I couldn't—"

"Kathryn is your woman, all right," Flandry said bitterly. "Prove to me that you're her man."

She was waiting at the airlock. The hours had circled her like wolves. He wished that his last sight of her could be without that anguish and exhaustion.

"Dominic?" she whispered.

"He agreed," Flandry told her. "You can go to him."

She swayed. He caught her and held her. "Now, now," he said clumsily, nigh to tears. He stroked the bright tousled hair. "Now, now, it's ended, we've won, you and I—" She slumped. He barely kept her from falling.

With the dear weight in his arms, he went to sickbay, laid her down and administered a stimulol injection. Color appeared in seconds, her lashes fluttered, the green eyes found him. She sat erect. "Dominic!" she cried. Weeping had harshened her voice. " 'Tis true?"

"See for yourself," he smiled. "Uh, take care, though. I gave you a minimum shot. You'll have a stiff metabolic price to pay as is."

She came to him, still weary and shaken. Their arms closed. They kissed for a long time.

"I wish," she said brokenly, "I almost wish—"

"Don't." He drew her head into the curve of his shoulder.

She stepped back. "Well, I wish you everything good there'll ever be, startin' with the girl who's really right for you."

"Thanks," he said. "Have no worries on my score. It's been worth any trouble I may have had," *and ever will have.* "Don't delay, Kathryn. Go to him."

She did. He sought the conn, where he could see the boat carry her off and await McCormac's technicians.

XVI

Strange suns enclouded *Persei*. A darkness aft hid the last glimpse of Imperial stars.

McCormac closed the suite door behind him. Kathryn rose. Rest, first under sedation, later under tranquilization, and medicine and nourishment had made her beautiful. She wore a gray shimmerlyn robe somebody had given her, open at throat and calf, sashed at the waist, smooth over the strong deep curves.

He stopped short. "I didn't expect you here yet!" he blurted.

"The medics released me," she answered, "seein' as how I'd come to happy news." Her smile was tremulous.

"Well . . . yes," he said woodenly. "We've verified that we shook those scouts dogging us, by our maneuvers inside that nebula. They'll never find us in uncharted interstellar space. Not that they'd want to, I'm sure. It'd be too risky, sending the power needed to deal with us as far as we're going. No, we're done with them, unless we return."

Shocked, she exclaimed: "You won't! You promised!"

"I know. Not that I mightn't—if—no, don't fear. I won't. Flandry was right, damn him, I'd have to raise allies, and those allies would have to be offered what it would split the Empire to give. Let's hope the threat that I *may* try again will force them to govern better . . . back there."

Her strickenness told him how much remained for her before the old calm strength was regained: "Dyuba, you'd think 'bout politics and fightin' in this hour?"

"I apologize," he said. "Nobody warned me you were coming. And I have been preoccupied."

She reached him, but they did not embrace. "That preoccupied?" she asked.

"Why, why, what do you mean? See here, you shouldn't be standing more than necessary. Let's get you seated. And, er, we'll have to arrange for the sleeping quarters to be remodeled—"

She closed her eyes briefly. When she opened them, she had command of herself. "Poor Hugh," she said. "You're scarred right badly too. I should've thought how you must've hurt."

"Nonsense." He urged her toward the couch.

She resisted in such a manner that his arms went around her. Laying hers about his neck and her cheek against his breast, she said, "Wait. You were tryin' to 'scape thinkin' 'bout us. 'Bout what I can be to you, after everything that was done. 'Bout whether the things I'm leavin' untold concernin' what passed 'tween Dominic and me, if they didn't include— But I've sworn they didn't."

"I cannot doubt you," rumbled through her.

"No, you're too honorable not to try hard to believe me, not to try hard to rebuild what we had. Poor Hugh, you're scared you might not be able."

"Well—associations, of course—" His clasp stiffened.

"I'll help you if you'll help me. I need it bad's you do."

"I understand," he said, gentler.

"No, you don't, Hugh," she replied gravely. "I realized the truth while I was alone, recuperatin', nothin' to do but think in a weird clear way till I'd fall asleep and the dreams came. I'm 'bout as well over what happened to me in the palace as I'll ever be. I'm the one to cure *you* of that. But you'll have to cure me of Dominic, Hugh."

"Oh, Kathryn!" he said into her hair.

"We'll try," she murmured. "We'll succeed, anyhow in part, anyhow enough to live. We must."

Vice Admiral Sir Ilya Kheraskov riffled the papers on his desk. The noise went from end to end of his office. Behind him, the projection screen today held an image of Saturn.

"Well," he said, "I've perused your account, and other relevant data, quite intensely since you arrived home. You were a busy young man, Lieutenant Commander."

"Yes, sir," said Flandry. He had taken a chair, but thought best to give the impression of sitting at attention.

"I regret leave was denied you and you've been made to spend the whole two weeks in Luna Prime. Must have been frustrating, the fleshpots of Terra glowing right overhead. But any number of irregularities had to be checked out."

"Yes, sir."

Kheraskov chuckled. "Stop worrying. We'll put you through assorted rituals, but I can tell you in confidence, you're off the hook and your brevet rank of commander will be made permanent. Till your next escapade gets you either broken or promoted, that is. I'd call the odds fifty-fifty."

Flandry leaned back. "Thank you, sir."

"You seem a touch disappointed," Kheraskov remarked. "Did you anticipate more?"

"Well, sir—"

Kheraskov cocked his head and grinned wider. "You ought to be effusive at me. I'm responsible for your getting this much. And I had to work for it!"

He drew breath. "True," he said, "your obtaining the code was an exploit which justifies overlooking a great deal else. But the else is such a very great deal. Besides losing *Asieneuve* on a trip most kindly described as reckless, you staged other performances which were high-handed at best, in gross excess of your authority at worst. Like removing the sector governor's prisoner on your own warrant; and conveying her with you; and concealing her presence on your return; and heading back out with her; and losing her to the enemy. . . . I'm afraid, Flandry, regardless of what rank you may gain, you'll never have another command."

That's no punishment. "Sir," Flandry said, "my report justifies whatever I did as according to regulations. So will the testimony of the men who served under me."

"Taking the most liberal interpretation of your discretionary rights that man, xeno, or computer can conceive of . . . yes, perhaps. But mainly, you rascal, I argued and politicked on your behalf because the Intelligence Corps needs you."

"Again I thank the admiral."

Kheraskov shoved the cigar box forward. "Take one," he said, "and show your gratitude by telling me what really happened."

Flandry accepted. "It's in my report, sir."

"Yes, and I know a weasel when one slinks by me. For instance—I read from the abstract of this wonderful document you wrote—ahem. 'Soon after leaving with Lady McCormac for Terra, with minimal crew for the sake of speed and secrecy as per orders, I was unfortunately noted and overhauled by an enemy cruiser which captured me. Brought to the flagship at Satan, I was surprised to find the rebels so discouraged that, upon learning Admiral Pickens had their code, they decided to flee the Empire. Lady McCormac prevailed upon them to spare me and my Didonian hand, leaving us behind with a disabled vessel. After the loyalists arrived, I discharged and returned home the said Didonian with the promised reward, then set course for Terra—' Well, no matter that." Kheraskov peered over the page. "Now what's the mathematical probability of a prowling cruiser just happening to come in detection range of you?"

"Well, sir," Flandry said, "the improbable has to happen sometimes. It's too bad the rebels wiped the computer's log in the course of removing my ship's hyperdrive. I'd have proof. But my account by itself ought to carry conviction."

"Yes, you build a very solid, interlocking pile of reasons, most of them unverifiable, why you had to do what you did and nothing else. You could spend your whole voyage back from Sector Alpha Crucis developing them. Be honest. You deliberately sought out Hugh McCormac and warned him about the code, didn't you?"

"Sir, that would have been high treason."

"Like doing away with a governor you didn't approve of? It's curious that he was last seen a short while before you cleared for departure."

"Much was going on, sir," Flandry said. "The city was in turmoil. His Excellency had personal enemies. Any one of them could have seen a chance to pay off scores. If the admiral suspects me of wrongdoing, he can institute proceedings to have me hypnoprobed."

Kheraskov sighed. "Never mind. You know I won't. For that matter, nobody's going to search after possible witnesses, rebels who may have elected to stay behind. Too big a job for too small a gain. As long as they keep their noses clean, we'll let them fade back into the general population. You're home free, Flandry. I'd simply hoped— But maybe it's best that I myself don't inquire too deeply. Do light your cigar. And we might send for a real potation. Do you like Scotch?"

"Love it, sir!" Flandry got the tobacco going and inhaled its perfume.

Kheraskov spoke an order on his intercom, leaned forward with elbows on desk, and blew clouds of his own. "Tell me one thing, though, prodigal son," he begged, "in exchange for my wholesale slaughter of fatted calves wearing stars and nebulas. Plain avuncular curiosity on my part. You have extended leave coming as soon as we can tie up the red tape. Where and how does your twisted ingenuity suggest you spend it?"

"Among those fleshpots the admiral mentioned," Flandry replied promptly. "Wine, women, and song. Especially women. It's been a long time."

Aside from such fun and forgetting, he thought while he grinned, *it will be the rest of my life.*

But she's happy. That's enough.

i/we remember.

The Feet is old now, slow to travel, aching in flesh when the mists creep around a longhouse that stands at the bottom of a winter night. The Wings that was of Many Thoughts is blind, and sits alone in his head save when a young one comes to learn. The Wings that was of Cave Discoverer and Woe is today in another of Thunderstone. The Hands of Many Thoughts and Cave Discoverer has long left his bones in the western mountains, whereto the Hands that was of Woe has long returned. Yet the memory lives. Learn, young Hands, of those who made oneness before i/we came to being.

It is more than the stuff of song, dance, and rite. No longer may We of this communion feel that Our narrow lands are the whole of the world. Beyond jungle and mountains is the sea; beyond heaven are those stars that Cave Discoverer dreamed of and Woe beheld. And there are the strangers with single bodies, they who visit Us rarely for trade and talk, but of whom We hear ever oftener as We in Our new search for enlightenment explore further among foreign communions. Their goods and their doings will touch Us more and more as the years pass, and will also make changes elsewhere than in Thunderstone, which changes will cause time to stream back across Us in different currents from that steadiness which i/we hitherto found easiest to imagine.

Beyond this and greater: How shall We achieve oneness with the whole world unless We understand it?

Therefore lie down at ease, young Hands, old Feet and Wings. Let wind, river, light, and time flow through. Be at rest, whole, in my/yourself, so gaining the strength that comes from peace, the strength to remember and to seek wisdom.

Be not afraid of the strangers with single bodies. Terrible are their powers, but those We can someday learn to wield like them if we choose. Rather pity that race, who are not beasts but can think, and thus know that they will never know oneness.

*One man's odyssey in an America
ravaged by nuclear war.*

ALFRED COPPEL

Dark December

**Begins where
DR. STRANGELOVE and FAIL SAFE
left off . . .**

Major Ken Gavin had only one thought when
peace was declared – had his wife and daughter in
California survived the onslaught of Russian
ICBMs?

Making his way slowly towards them with whatever
transport he can commandeer, Gavin witnesses
the full horror of the holocaust – grotesque craters
where towns used to be, the ever-present odour of
death and disease and, most sinister of all, the
recourse of the surviving populace to tribal,
vigilante ways. Driven forward by a powerful,
innate homing instinct, Gavin survives all this
and goes on to a reunion which is at once tragic
and triumphant.

*This account of one man's reaction when the
unthinkable happens with unspeakable results is an
unforgettable reading experience.*

EDMUND COOPER

KRONK

'Mad ... original ... satirical ... extremely funny'

P939 – the greatest venereal disease in the history of mankind

The day Gabriel Chrome, a failed book sculptor contemplating his suicide on the Thames Embankment, stumbled on the suicide bid of the naked Camilla Greylaw, was a day of hopeful redemption for a corrupt and violent world.

For the lovely form that he chanced to preserve was the sole carrier of a contagious venereal disease. A bug which could inhibit the aggressive instinct, rendering total placidity in all humans.

At once Gabriel's life has new meaning and purpose. To save mankind becomes his hardened ambition. But mankind seems far from hope.

'Mr. Cooper takes a brisk succession of targets, and manages to smack most of them on the nose'
Financial Times

'He writes with great authority and skill'
Arthur C. Clarke

GREAT SCIENCE FICTION FROM CORONET BOOKS

Poul Anderson
☐ 16480 8 **THE ENEMY STARS**   25p

Algis Budrys
☐ 04399 7 **THE IRON THORN**   20p

Edmund Cooper
☐ 15091 2 **THE LAST CONTINENT**   25p
☐ 15132 3 **THE UNCERTAIN MIDNIGHT**   25p
☐ 10904 1 **FIVE TO TWELVE**   25p
☐ 16217 1 **KRONK**   30p

ed. Idella Purnell Stone
☐ 12731 7 **14 GREAT TALES OF E.S.P.**   30p

Kurt Vonnegut jnr
☐ 02876 9 **THE SIRENS OF TITAN**   30p

John Wyndham
☐ 15834 4 **THE SECRET PEOPLE**   30p
☐ 15835 2 **STOWAWAY TO MARS**   30p

ed. Groff Conklin
☐ 02880 7 **SEVEN COME INFINITY**   17½p

Alfred Coppel
☐ 14809 8 **DARK DECEMBER**   25p

All these books are available at your bookshop or newsagent, or
can be ordered direct from the publisher. Just tick the titles you
want and fill in the form below.

CORONET BOOKS, Cash Sales Department, Kernick Industrial Estate, Penryn, Cornwall.

Please send cheque or postal order, no currency, and allow 7p per
book (6p per book on orders of five copies and over) to cover the
cost of postage and packing in U.K., 7p per copy overseas.

Name ....

Address ....

....